DARK ENTRY

JOHN B. KACHUBA

John B. Kachuba

HELLBENDER BOOKS

an imprint of Sunbury Press, Inc.
Mechanicsburg, PA USA

HELLBENDER BOOKS

an imprint of Sunbury Press, Inc.
Mechanicsburg, PA USA

For information about special discounts for bulk purchases, please contact Sunbury Press Orders Dept. at (855) 338-8359 or orders@sunburypress.com.

To request one of our authors for speaking engagements or book signings, please contact Sunbury Press Publicity Dept. at publicity@sunburypress.com.

ISBN: 978-1-62006-029-2 (Trade paperback)

Library of Congress Control Number: 2018953060

FIRST HELLBENDER BOOKS EDITION: September 2018

Product of the United States of America
0 1 1 2 3 5 8 13 21 34 55

Set in Bookman Old Style
Designed by Crystal Devine
Cover by Lawrence Knorr
Edited by Lawrence Knorr

Continue the Enlightenment!

For Ethan

1868

The Reverend Phelps never liked coming up the mountain to Dudleytown. It wasn't just the steep climb up the narrow twisting road to the village that bothered him, although at his advanced age, he sometimes thought that hike would kill him, but his unease was caused more by the villagers themselves. They were a rough lot, taciturn and obstinate in their ways. Rarely did they descend from Coltsfoot Mountain and that was just fine with the people that lived in the flatlands below—the same people that coerced their misbehaving children into obedience by threatening to send them up the mountain to the Dudleytown bogeymen if they didn't mind their manners.

If his sister Lucinda had not married one of the Dudleytown charcoal burners, against his advice, of course, he would not now be trekking up the mountain, sweating beneath the warm July sun. There were spots of shade along his route on Dark Entry Road that offered some comfort, but much of the mountain had been denuded of trees, felled by the villagers for the making of charcoal. In the open areas alongside the road, he could see several huge piles of smoldering wood and the sooty men who tended them. Some of them stood high atop the mounds wielding long poles. Smoke was thick in the air, filling his lungs, the acrid odor burning his nostrils. His eyes watered in the pungent air. How could these people live up here, he wondered for perhaps the thousandth time. No sane man would want to be a charcoal burner.

Poor Lucinda. What a life she could have had. He never understood what she saw in Quentin Randolph, but whatever

1

it was, it was enough to make her reject the schoolmaster's marriage proposal—a much better match, Phelps thought—and run off to Dudleytown with Randolph. And what had she gained? A tiny house atop a mountain and a silent and moody man with a violent temper. Poor Lucinda. Were it not for her young son and the fact that she was the youngest of all his siblings, the one he thought most in need of care, he would have left her to her wild mountain man. But nothing less than his Christian duty moved him to look in on her and the boy now and then, as he was doing now, beneath a sun that seemed to be growing hotter with each step he took.

He passed a few small cottages nestled among the trees, simple dwellings that seemed to spring up from the earth. They were unpainted, although moss grew on some of them, covering them in green like exotic plants taking root beneath the trees. He saw no one at the houses.

At last, he arrived at the end of Dark Entry Road. A small track led off to the right. His sister's house lay off that path, but he could not proceed because a horse-drawn wagon was creaking up the track. The wagon was filled with charcoal and the man who sat on the wagon seat was black with grime and soot. Phelps stood aside as the wagon approached, the unsmiling driver giving the reverend a barely perceptible nod of his head as he passed.

Phelps walked down the track and arrived at Lucinda's house. Hers was newer than the others and had not yet been attacked by the surrounding vegetation, except for a fragrant honeysuckle bush that pushed itself up against one side of the house. He stepped up on the stone doorstep and rapped on the door.

No answer.

He knocked again, louder this time.

The house remained silent.

"Lucinda?"

She did not reply.

He tried the door and found that it was unlocked. He pushed the door open and stepped inside.

"Lucinda?"

The small parlor in which he stood, his hat in his hand, was dim, only a meager ray of sunshine entering the room from a little window at the back. Nothing seemed amiss in the room; there was the rocker by the hearth, a round table with two chairs, an oil lamp upon the table. Dried bunches of herbs hung from the rafters.

The door to the bedroom was closed.

Phelps walked over to it and tapped on the door. "Lucinda?" he said, softly, "it's me, Thomas." No answer. "Quentin?" He turned the knob and slowly pushed the door open.

The room was darker than the parlor, the shade drawn down over the single window, so it took his eyes a few moments to adjust to the low light. Lucinda's body lay upon the bed clad in a blood-soaked white nightgown. A bloody ax lay like a lover on the bed beside her. Lucinda's head looked up at him from the floor.

He gagged, staggering against the doorframe. He felt dizzy, liable to faint. His heart pounded, and he could hardly catch his breath. Somehow, he found his way out of the house and leaned against the wall, trying to suck in fresh air, but tasting only the poisoned air from the charcoal fires. He fell to his knees, the gorge rising within him, and he heaved into the weeds, coughing and sputtering. After a few moments, he recovered and rose to his feet.

Quentin, it must have been Quentin! And where was the boy? Anger and fear burst inside him simultaneously. His legs still shaky, he forced himself to move. He noticed the barn behind the house and saw the door was open. Quentin must be inside, he thought. He stalked toward the barn, his rage conquering his fear of the man.

"Quentin!"

He reached the barn and hesitated only a moment before entering.

Quentin was inside the barn. He hung by his neck from a rope tied around a rafter, his face swollen like a purple watermelon, his eyes popped out of his head. A ladder lay on the dirt floor beneath his gently swaying body.

The Reverend Phelps once again fell to his knees.

ONE

Sandy Lawrence was not a reckless driver, but it was a thrill for her to mash the accelerator of her blue BMW as she drove up Route 7. The narrow, winding road, flanked by tall pines and hemlocks, offered a tricky test for any driver willing to push her limits. And Sandy was willing to push her limits.

With the convertible top down, the July sun warmed her as she flew in and out of shady patches on the road. The wind tugged at the Yankees ball cap covering her long blonde hair, threatening to send it sailing into the dark woods lining the road. She glanced to her right and saw the broad expanse of the Housatonic River, glistening green in the sunlight. The road ran parallel to the river, hugging its curves north through Connecticut and into Massachusetts, but Sandy wouldn't be driving any further than Coltsfoot Mountain. At the speed she was driving, it wouldn't take her long to reach her destination unless, of course, some county mountie stopped her.

She barreled into a turn in the road, saw a squirrel sitting there nonchalantly working on a nut, and swerved the car at the last second, missing the animal by a hair.

"Damn!" She slammed on the brakes, pulling the car back into the right lane and slowing it down.

She pulled into a gravel turnoff, shutting off the engine, shaking. She sat there for a moment looking straight ahead, vaguely aware of the birds twittering in the pine branches overhead. Then she lost it. The tears came again, as they had so many times before over the last few weeks, and she couldn't stop them. There was no other traffic on this lonely stretch of highway, nobody to see, and she let the tears fall.

She didn't want to think about Kevin again, but there was no stopping her mind, no blocking out the thoughts that had plagued her since she had finally realized that a man with a drug habit and a mercurial temperament would never be the kind of man with whom she could have the relationship she so badly wanted, she so badly needed. Walking out on him, this time forever she told herself, had not been easy. Knowing how he could be, she had left their apartment in New York when he was at work in his midtown photography studio. She didn't take much with her; some clothes, her laptop, a few small personal items—including a teddy bear given to her by one of her clients—and that was it. Minutes later, she was on the Hutchinson Parkway heading for Connecticut.

Leslie had been a darling and had offered her the use of a second home she owned on Coltsfoot Mountain. The only friend in whom Sandy could confide, Leslie had heard all about the trouble between Sandy and Kevin. She promised to keep Sandy's whereabouts a secret, should he ever come looking for her.

She opened the glove box and took out some tissues, dabbing at her eyes. She was doing the right thing, the smart thing, in leaving Kevin, but that didn't ease her pain. The problem was that she loved him, despite his problems. That was irrational. She knew that, unless he sought professional help, Kevin would never change. Life with him would only get worse, instead of better, no matter what she did. She could not change him if he didn't want to change himself. She knew all these things, and Leslie continually reminded her of them, and still, she loved the man. She was a fool. Pathetic. Needy. Even now, she was tempted to turn the car around and drive back to New York, drive back to Kevin.

The shade in which the car sat beneath the pines was cool, almost chilly. A cold breeze sprung up from the woods and with it came a memory, as though the cold swept from her mind everything else. The memory was not a pleasant one. She recalled a time when Kevin had been unusually anxious about a big assignment he was hoping to get from a major department store in the city. He hadn't heard any-thing for a few days after showing the marketing manager his portfolio and he was on edge. Cocaine helped take the edge off. A lot of cocaine. Sandy didn't like the mania she saw in him when he was high like that and she told him so. Kevin became angry. That was the first time he had ever hit her. She could explain away his behavior by chalking it up to stress. It wasn't much of a blow. Just a quick slap, noth-ing like the beat-up wives you saw on *Cops* or read about in the tabloids. No, nothing at all like those low-lifes.

Still, in her more rational moments, she saw it. Kevin had hit her.

That was why she was now sitting in her car in the woods of Connecticut, crying. "Stop it, girl," she said aloud. "Get a grip!"

She wiped the tears from her eyes and threw the tissue on the floor. She tilted the rearview mirror to get a better look at her face. Her blue eyes were still damp with tears and red-rimmed. "Great," she said, "now I look like *I'm* on crack." She tugged on the bill of her Yankees hat, making sure it was secure, started the car and pulled back onto the roadway.

She felt better after her crying spell. She concentrated on her driving and on the lush scenery flashing by. She slowed down as she drove through the village of Kent with its little shops, then picked up speed again, passing through Kent Furnace and Bull's Bridge. She was getting closer to Corn-wall Bridge and Coltsfoot Mountain.

She had been to Leslie's house on the mountain only once before. It was shortly after Leslie's father died and she had inherited the house. The two women spent a quiet weekend there, blissfully doing nothing at all except relaxing and en-joying each other's company.

Leslie had reminded Sandy that the road up the moun-tain was not easy to find, so she slowed down as she came into Cornwall Bridge and saw the red covered bridge span-ning the river. A hundred yards or so further and she saw the rusted sign, partly obscured by a huge maple tree, that read *Dark Entry Road-Private*. She was there.

She turned onto the narrow gravel road. Trees crowded up to the edge of the road and so many large branches arched overhead that she felt as though she was driving through an emerald tunnel. There were no other cars on the road and that was a good thing since it was so narrow that one would have to pull over into the trees to let another car pass. It was much cooler beneath the tree canopy and darker, with the sun finding only a few holes here and there in the foliage. Dark Entry alright, she thought.

The woods on either side of the road were thick and impenetrable. It seemed like night in the woods although it was only mid-afternoon. She drove slowly, trying not to bang the chassis too hard on the rutted gravel road. Other than the noise of the engine and the gravel crunching beneath the tires, it was strangely quiet as she ascended the mountain. No wind. No birds. There were also no houses visible anywhere along the road. She remembered that it was that way when she had stayed there with Leslie, but that had been several years ago. She was surprised that more people had not built summer homes on the mountain.

Finally, the road leveled out and came to a dead-end. There was the house.

In a small clearing in the woods stood a large A-frame house. The façade was almost entirely glass. She could see part of a deck at the rear of the house, which she recalled offered spectacular views of the woods. There was a small driveway into which she pulled the BMW.

She got out of the car and was immediately surrounded by silence. She stood there looking at the house, its large windows dark in the shade of the trees. Some women might be afraid to stay alone in such a house, in such a place, she thought, but she was not. She liked to push her limits and perhaps, she would be pushing them here. No, she had nothing to fear from the location. She had only to fear her own mind. As if that wasn't bad enough.

She found the key in a little metal box inside a planter on the front step, just where Leslie said it would be. She stepped inside, dropped her bags on the hardwood floor and walked down two steps into the living room. At the rear of the house, windows soared from floor to ceiling, offering her a panoramic view of the little clearing behind the house and the dark woods beyond that. Fully leafed out, the trees formed a massive green wall around the house, creating a natural fortress with her the princess in the tower. Or was she an inmate in a prison? No, she wouldn't think like that; this was a getaway, a place of refuge while she got her life back together.

The living room was the largest room in the house, clearly designed to be the main gathering area. Two large couches were canted toward the view outside, a blue and gold Persian rug on the oak floor between them. A ceiling fan hung suspended from the exposed rafters angling up high above her and two more rugs in faux Native American designs were draped over the rail along the loft. Sandy remembered that there was a bed in the open loft and she decided she would sleep there, rather than in the small bedroom on the ground floor which Leslie used when she visited the house.

The sun was low in the sky and the shadows of dusk were already creeping through the woods. She turned on a few lights, retrieved her bags from the entry and brought them upstairs to the loft. There was a small dresser beside the bed and she carelessly tossed her clothes from the bags into the drawers. She sat her laptop on the dresser beside a clock radio and plugged it into the wall outlet. She sat on the bed, staring at the little red battery light. She really should check her email, she thought. Perhaps one of her clients was trying to contact her. She should check, shouldn't she?

"Come on, sweetie," she said, aloud. "Who are you trying to kid? It's a message from Kevin that you really want."

She sighed. Just as she was about to give in and reach for the computer, loud music suddenly blasted into the loft. She yelped, jumping to her feet. "What the hell?" The clock radio pumped out nasty rap music and she grabbed it, turning it off. She noticed that the alarm had been set, for whatever reason, at 5 PM, no doubt by some other visitor. How many days had the music played in the empty house, she wondered. It was strange to think of that awful music filling this house in the woods each day for an hour with its hateful, misogynistic lyrics, and with no one to hear it other than the squirrels.

Still rattled from the unexpected intrusion into her solitude, Sandy went back downstairs. She flopped onto one of the couches, curling her legs up beneath her. She watched the last of the sun's rays glinting through the trees like burning red embers and before she knew it, the darkness of night covered the house. She felt chilled and drew a comforter up over her legs. There was a stone fireplace on the opposite wall, but she felt too lazy to build a fire, even though a stack of firewood sat on the hearth.

The hearth reminded her of the fireplace in the room she and Kevin had shared at an eighteenth-century bed-and-breakfast in the Berkshires. It was in December, just a week or two before Christmas and a fresh snowfall covered the ground and pine trees, making them look like droopy ghosts. After a walk in the little town, kicking up fresh snow as they went, their breath steaming in the frosty air, they came back to their room where a warm fire was already crackling in the fireplace. Without a word needing to be said, they peeled off their clothes and snuggled under the blankets piled high upon the four-poster bed. Okay, it was more than snuggling. Kevin, at times, could be very romantic and that was one of those times.

She felt her eyes becoming moist. How could it all go so wrong?

She wiped her eyes and looked out the window. A pale light was inching its way across the grass in the clearing. As she watched, the sharp rim of the moon slowly began to rise above the trees, casting their shadows across the clearing. A full moon. She loved watching the moon and a full moon on her first night there was a nice surprise. Consider it a gift, she thought.

She felt a jolt at her hip and heard an electronic buzz. It sounded one more time before she was able to extract her cell phone from her pocket. She looked at the number on the screen before she answered: Leslie.

"Les!"

"Hey, Sandy, how are you doing? Did you get there alright?"

"Yes, no problem. Thanks again, I really needed to get away."

"I know you did, honey. Do you have everything you need?"

An ironic question, she thought. "Sure, I'm fine."

"Okay." There was a pause on the other end and Sandy could almost hear her friend's mind working through the phone. "Listen, Sandy," she said, "what do you want me to say if Kevin should call me? You know that might be likely."

"Yes. I don't know, Les. I don't want to talk to him today, that's for sure, but what about tomorrow, or the day after? I don't see any way that I can make our situation better, but what if he really wants to change?"

"What if he does?"

"God, I don't know. Am I really that stupid?"

"No, you're not."

Sandy drew the comforter up over her chest. The full moon was now visible, seemingly balanced upon the tip of a tall hemlock. It looked like it could roll down the sloping branches of the tree at any moment.

"I need to think things through, Les. I had to get away from him, that much was certain, but what happens next, I can't tell."

"What does your heart tell you?"

"I think my heart's on vacation, but my gut tells me that I need to protect myself."

"Okay, fair enough. So, I take it you don't want me to say anything to him if he calls me."

"I think that's best."

"Fine, but he does know about my Connecticut house. He may be able to figure out where you went. What then?"

That thought caused her to glance out the window into the darkness beyond. "We'll just have to wait and see."

"I'm worried about you, sweetie."

Sandy smiled. "I know you are. You're a dear friend and I'm grateful for all your help. Don't worry about me, I'll be fine."

"You're sure?"

"Yes."

"Alright, but don't be surprised if I check in on you from time to time."

"I would like it if you did, Les."

After Leslie hung up, Sandy lay on the couch watching the moon slowly arc across the night sky. Emotionally drained, she felt as though she could not lift her body from off the couch and so, eyes closing on moonlight, she drifted off to sleep.

TWO

Sunlight already filled the room when she opened her eyes the next morning. She sat up on the couch and threw off the comforter. She walked over to the window and stood looking out. The sun sparkled in the trees, showering them in fiery emeralds. A planter on the deck held a geranium plant, its scarlet blossoms standing out in stark relief against the dark green leaves. Two *chaise longues* sat on the deck, a small round table between them. Leslie must have been out to the house not too long ago. Beyond the deck was a clearing, not a lawn as such, but closer to a natural meadow, with long grass and a sprinkling of wildflowers. The deep woods lay about twenty yards beyond the clearing.

She opened the door and stepped out onto the deck. In full sunshine, the wooden deck was warm beneath her bare feet. There was a small thermometer mounted on the wall that already read seventy-two degrees. It would be a warm day.

She went back inside and headed for the kitchen. She was desperately in need of coffee. There wasn't much by way of food in the cupboards—she made a mental note to go to the grocery in town later that day—but, thank God, there was coffee. She started up the coffee maker and while it was brewing, went upstairs to the loft. Digging a pair of denim shorts out of the dresser, she shucked off her jeans and put on the shorts. By the time she came downstairs again, the coffee was ready.

Sandy poured the steaming coffee into a blue mug emblazoned with *Rabbit Hill Coffee House,* whatever that was. She found a package of Graham crackers that seemed reasonably fresh and took her breakfast out to the deck. Settled in a *chaise*, she sipped her coffee and munched on the crackers.

This was so different from grabbing a cappuccino at Starbucks, waiting on line in the crowded store, buses and taxis creeping by bumper to bumper in the congested street. Although she worked at home when she was designing a Web page, she was often out and about in the city as she met with prospective clients and tried to convince them that a Sandy Lawrence designed Website was exactly what they needed for their business to become successful. She was good at what she did, both in the design work and the sales component and she made a decent living at it, even in New York City.

This was definitely not New York, she thought, as she relaxed on the deck, watching the trees gently swaying in an almost intangible breeze. The quiet here was deafening. She was surprised that she did not hear or see any birds. Perhaps it was already too warm for them and they were simply lying low, "just chillin'," as Kevin would say.

No, no Kevin, she reminded herself. Not today.

She ate one last cracker and placed the package on the table. As unfamiliar as the silence was to her, it felt good, as did the sun pouring its warmth over her. She finished her coffee and set the mug on the table with the crackers. She closed her eyes and lay back on the *longue*, letting the sun wash over her.

She lay there for a while, her eyes closed, letting her mind relax, feeling the tension in her body float away. The sun felt wonderful. After a few minutes, beads of perspiration formed on her forehead. She sat up and stripped off her tank top. There wasn't much to the bra she wore, but women wore even less at the beach. Besides, she thought, there was no one around to see her. She lay down again, letting the sun caress her body. She felt herself letting go, her body sinking down into the *longue* as the warn fingers of sunshine stroked her body. Her mind drifted, fleeting images flitting by like an old-time newsreel. She could make no sense of them; no sooner would her mind focus on one, then it disappeared, replaced by yet another entirely different image. Perhaps she dreamed, she didn't know, but the parade of images warned her deep inside and made her feel good.

Without any conscious volition on her part, some of the images seemed to coalesce and became more intense. There was a man, she thought, maybe Kevin, maybe not, she couldn't tell. She heard no words but had the notion that he was trying to communicate with her. He seemed intent upon reaching her and she felt a shiver of sexual tension race through her. Now, the hot rays of sunshine touching her body truly felt like warm hands stroking her, exploring her, and she squirmed a little on the *longue*.

Kevin. She was dreaming, and it was Kevin touching her as only he knew how to touch her, as she wanted to be touched. She gave up trying to understand, trying to make sense of what she was feeling. She simply let it happen. Through the thin material of her bra, she felt his fingers on her breast, teasing her in a way that brought a sigh to her lips.

But then, as though something lost deep within her had come awake, she suddenly saw that it was Kevin touching her, but not Kevin, not really, that it was someone, something else entirely and that whoever, whatever, was not a good thing. Her breath came rapidly, her heart thudded. She strained her body away from the alien touch, finally jerking awake on the *longue*. She was perspiring, the cold sweat of fear.

My god! What the hell was that?

Despite the sunlight filtering through the trees, the woods now seemed secretive and sinister. Could there be eyes out there, watching her? She snatched up her tank top and yanked it over her head, grabbed the cup and crackers from the table and hastened back into the house, locking the door behind her.

She felt better, once she was inside. Her breathing slowed, her heart returned to a normal rhythm. She looked out into the clearing and saw nothing unusual, nothing to fear. She laughed at her silly dream. You've got to get a grip on yourself, Sandy, she told herself. You'll make yourself crazy if you don't.

He liked nothing better than to spend his time wandering over Coltsfoot Mountain. There wasn't a path he didn't know through the deep woods and he created his own paths as well. He knew the mountain better than anyone else. Of course, he never spoke to anyone else because no one was aware he lived upon the mountain, and that was the way he wanted it. There were some that had accidentally discovered him, but they all came to a bad end, and so, he remained only a rumored ghost to the people in the town below.

He could not remember when he first came to the mountain or how he got there. It seemed to him that he had always been there and that he would be forever. He knew that his animal friends died—he often came across their carcasses in the woods—but somehow, such an end did not seem possible for him.

He didn't mind being alone, but it made him nervous when hikers or teenagers from the town below came up to the mountain. He kept his eyes on them, watching them from the safety of the woods.

He also watched the house atop the mountain.

Usually, the house was empty, dark glass eyes gazing into the woods. Sometimes though, there was a lady with brown hair living in the house. Curious about her, he had entered the house several times when she was not around and left without leaving a trace of his presence. But now, there was a new lady there, a lady with yellow hair. He called her Yellow Lady and called the other simply Lady.

He had not been near the house for several days, staying closer to his tiny shack nestled in a wooded ravine. But only this morning he had wandered near the clearing and saw the Yellow Lady on the deck behind the house. He was surprised to see anyone there, especially someone he had never seen before.

He watched her from the safety of the woods.

Yellow Lady was pretty. He crouched in the bushes, watching her, fascinated. Her hair was long and yellow. He wondered what it would feel like to pet it. Soft, he imagined. He didn't know how long he watched her—time meant nothing to him—but, after a while, she sat up and took off her shirt. He felt a lump in his throat as she lay back down. He continued to watch her, entranced. There was something about her that seemed familiar, precious, and for a moment he thought he heard a woman softly singing. He held his breath and listened, but the singing disappeared, leaving him with a sensation all at once both pleasurable and frightening. He never felt this way when he observed Lady. No, Yellow Lady was special. He didn't know how, only that she was. That thought made his heart run like a scared rabbit. He had been told there were women with special powers, powers that could charm you or hurt you. He remembered hearing stories about such magic women, although he could not remember who told them to him. Was Yellow Lady one of those women?

He hid in the bushes gazing at her when, suddenly, she sat up as if frightened by something. She snatched up her shirt and hurried into the house. Had she seen him? No, that was impossible, he thought, no one ever sees him.

For a few moments, she stood inside the house by the door. Then, she disappeared into the dark interior. He waited to see if she would return. When she did not, he silently crept away, headed for the shelter of his shack on the other side of the mountain.

All the way home, Yellow Lady burned in his mind like a flash of lightning.

THREE

Sandy smiled at the sign over the weathered building that read *Buxton's General Store.* It was difficult to believe that there were still places in Connecticut that had general stores, but Cornwall Bridge was one of those places. In smaller print below the store's name, the sign read, *Ned Buxton, Prop.* Really. Ned? She felt like she had just walked onto the set of *Green Acres.*

Quaint or not, she needed to buy some groceries and Buxton's was the only place for miles around to do that. She drove slowly down Dark Entry Road as she descended the mountain. The day was hot, so she drove with the convertible top down. She thought about the dream she had had earlier that morning. Now, in the warm air, with the bright sun streaming through the trees, she laughed at herself and realized how ridiculous it was to be spooked by a dream. Yes, it was weird and frightening, but it was a dream, simple as that. No reason to get her knickers in a bunch over something that stupid.

Driving through the old red covered bridge spanning the Housatonic River, she easily found a parking space right in front of the store. The store was larger than it looked from the outside. Inside, there was an old wood floor, scarred and scratched by countless shoppers over the years, and the aisles were narrow and crowded together. She took one of the three shopping carts at the front of the store and pushed it leisurely through the aisles; she was in no hurry. There were only a few other people in the store, one of them a pimply-faced kid stacking up cans of Alpo dog food.

She didn't know how long she would stay at Leslie's house, probably not too long, so she kept her list short; bread, pasta, some fruit and produce, a few canned goods and, of course, more coffee. That should do it. She could always come back if she decided to stay longer. If.

She pushed the cart to the checkout at the front of the store. The bald man behind the counter looked as old and weathered as the store. He wore a denim shirt with the name *Ned* embroidered in red above the pocket. So, there really was a Ned Buxton, Prop, she thought.

"Find everything okay?" he asked, as he began ringing up her purchases.

"Yes, fine."

He smiled and nodded his head. "I know the shelves are a bit crowded. I've been saying I should expand the store, but I've been saying that for the last thirty-five years. Don't look like I'll get around to it at this point."

Not likely. The man must have been in his eighties already.

He placed the tomatoes she had bought on a scale and squinted at the number through his glasses. "That your car?" He nodded toward the BMW visible through the window. He removed the tomatoes from the scale.

"Yes."

"Nice. Sporty. I bet it drives like a dream."

"Yes, it does, although I have to be careful on some of the roads around here," she said. "I thought I'd break an axle driving on Dark Entry Road."

He paused, one hand holding open the brown paper bag, the other holding a can of beans. "Dark Entry Road?"

She nodded. "I'm staying on the mountain for a little awhile, at a friend's house."

"The O'Neil place." He slowly placed the can in the bag, his eyes never leaving her face.

"Yes, that's right. Do you know it?"

"It's the only house up there. I knew Ted O'Neil, a great guy."

He continued to bag her groceries. He didn't rush, but there was no one else in line anyway, so she didn't mind.

Besides, he seemed like a nice enough man and she was happy to talk with someone other than herself. "His daughter Leslie is my friend."

"Didn't know her that well, but I knew Ted and I'd been up on that mountain with him more than a few times." He leaned over the counter toward her and looked around as if he had a secret to reveal to her. "Are you alone up there?" he asked, in a low voice. She paused, uncertain if she should answer that question or not. "I know, I know, it's none of my business," he said, raising his hands. "It's just that, when I see a young lady like you, I see my own daughters and I guess I would worry about them up there."

Sandy's unease about his motives in asking that question disappeared, but now she wondered why he was so concerned about her. After all, she was not one of his daughters; she was a stranger to him. "Why would you worry, Mister Buxton?"

He had bagged the last of the groceries and rang up the total on the register. "It's nothing, really. I'm just an old worrier. Forget it. I'm sure you can take care of yourself."

She noted how his tone had changed, just as a young woman with a squirming toddler sitting in the cart entered the checkout line behind her. Sandy had the impression that there was more the old man wanted to tell her, but that he could not say anything while other people were around.

"That'll be fifty-four dollars and thirty cents," Ned said, with a big smile.

She paid him and scooped up the two paper bags.

"Thanks for shopping at Buxton's," he called after her, as she exited the store. "And good luck."

Those two words echoed in her mind as she drove back up the mountain. Why would he worry about her? Really, it couldn't be anything more than his fatherly concern for her. He was just that kind of guy, a warm, fuzzy grandfatherly type of guy. He simply wished her well, just as he would wish his own daughters well.

Still, *good luck*?

Kevin shifted the weight of his camera bag on one shoulder and turned the key in the lock of the apartment door. It always stuck so, with his free shoulder, he gave the door a nudge. Inside, he carefully placed the bag upon the couch. He looked around. Everything was as he had left it that morning. Sandy had not returned.

It had only been two days since she left, not long enough for him to worry about her. She was an independent woman, and she would be fine on her own, wherever she was. She just needed some time. She'd cool off soon and when she did, she would come back, he was certain. It wasn't the first time she had left him and each time she came back, just like a retriever, he thought, and laughed.

He walked into the bedroom, which no longer held the scent of her perfume, although the well-worn indentation on her side of the bed was still evident. Why did he still sleep on his side of the bed, he wondered. He kicked off his Nikes. He shrugged off his clothes, stepped into the shower and let the hot water cascade over his body. As he soaped himself down, he was aware of the firm muscles beneath his fingers, the flat belly. He may be nearing forty, but he was still in damn good shape, he thought. There were other women that would gladly give themselves to him—he sometimes had offers—and he also knew Sandy was a passionate and physical woman; she'd be back for more.

"Once you've had Kevin Perillo, no one else will do," he said, laughing.

Opening the shampoo bottle, he washed his thick hair and his neatly trimmed beard. He soaked in the hot steam for a few more minutes before stepping out of the shower and toweling himself dry.

He dressed in tan pants and an ivory colored silk shirt. Sitting on the edge of the bed, he pulled on a pair of Dr. Martens shearling boots. Kevin stood before the mirror above the dresser and decided that he needed the little gold pendant Sandy had given him for his birthday two years ago to complete his ensemble. It was a small square tablet with unidentifiable symbols engraved upon it. Sandy said that it was called the pendant of Machu Picchu and that it was supposed to have protective powers. They both laughed at that since neither one of them were superstitious and Sandy admitted that she bought it for him simply because it was pretty. He placed it around his neck, satisfied with how it looked nestled in the neckline of his shirt.

He paused before the mirror, checking his reflection, making sure he looked good enough to go out. Yes, he was a bit vain about his appearance, he admitted that, but shouldn't a person always try to look his best? What was wrong with that? Sandy sometimes teased him about his "primping," as she called it, but that was easy for her to say. She was blessed with a natural beauty that required little care, the kind of beauty that other women instantly recognized and envied. Yet, for all of that, she seemed almost unaware of the effect she had on men and women alike. Men wanted her, women resented her.

He thought that he was lucky he had found her, although there were times when they did not get along. The cocaine, for example. She was all over his case about his using cocaine, despite that she wasn't averse to a taste or two; she was no saint. It had been a long time since she had used it, that was true, and she had only used it infrequently, but she simply did not understand the feeling he got from cocaine. He had more energy, he felt more alert, more alive. He thought of cocaine as something like a super-vitamin, a way to perk up after a draining day at work. She thought he was becoming addicted to the stuff, which was ridiculous. He could stop at any time if he so desired. Any time.

While he was thinking of it, he opened the top drawer of the dresser and removed a little Ziploc bag containing white powder. Just in case.

He walked into the living room, put on a black leather jacket, slipped the plastic bag into an inner pocket, and left the apartment, making sure the door was locked securely behind him. Sandy had her keys and could let herself in when she returned.

Meanwhile, dinner. He walked several blocks to a favorite restaurant, a little Italian place called *Theresa's*. He liked eating there because, number one, the food was great, and, number two, it was quiet and intimate, rarely crowded. It offered him a period of calm before a night of partying.

He found a booth in the back corner of the restaurant. The light in the restaurant was low, romantic he guessed. A single red candle stuck in an empty Chianti *flasco* glowed upon the table. Kitschy. He had been there often enough to recognize some of the servers, but the young woman who now handed him a menu was new.

She smiled at him. "Just one?"

"Yes, unfortunately," he said, smiling back at her.

"Would you like to hear our specials tonight?" He nodded, and she began to recite the list of specials.

He appraised her as she spoke. Her face was delicate and angular, her eyes blue. She wore her long dark hair pulled back in a ponytail and tied with a white ribbon. She was slim—not as voluptuous as Sandy—but her body was shapely in the black jeans and shirt.

"Thank you," he said, when she had completed the list. "I'm sorry, what was your name?"

"Crystal."

"Thank you, Crystal. Why don't you give me a few minutes to look over the menu? In the meantime, you can bring me a scotch and water."

"Coming up," she said.

He admired the sway of her hips and the curvature of her derriere as she walked away. The night was looking up already.

FOUR

She had already spent two nights at the house on the mountain and, while she had enjoyed the peace and serenity there, she also missed the society of other people. Sandy was a city girl, without question, and there was only so much country life that she could accept.

Of course, it was not the city from which she was escaping, it was Kevin.

But was she really escaping? Perhaps, that remained to be seen. She knew only too well what Kevin had become and she didn't like it. Still, she would be a liar if she said that she didn't think about better days with him, if she said that she didn't miss him.

She tried not to think too much about him, tried to let the tranquility of this isolated house work some magic in her. Thankfully, she had brought her laptop with her so that she could continue to work. She smiled to herself as she thought of her pragmatic nature. Even in a state of emotional distress, she remembered to bring work with her.

Now, as she sat on the *chaise* on the deck, working at her laptop, she was glad she had brought it. She was having difficulty coming up with the right approach for a Web site she was designing for one of her clients. The TotToy Company was a small company that made very expensive toys for very spoiled children. F.A.O. Schwartz kind of toys. Why any child would need a $500 teddy bear was beyond her comprehension. The stupid little thing sat beside her, given to her by the TotToy people for "inspiration." She thought of her own favorite childhood teddy, a gnarly-looking black bear she had named "Tubby." That bear probably cost her parents only a few dollars, but she loved it, playing the hell out of it. Tattered and worn, one ear hanging by a thread, Tubby had eventually been exiled to the attic where, no doubt, he still slept hidden in one of the many boxes her mother stored there. Poor Tubby. One of these days, she just might go and rescue him.

She fiddled around with some images of the TotToy bears, moving them here and there on the page, but they just didn't look right. Something was missing; what was it?

Her cell phone rang, breaking her concentration.

It was Leslie. Sandy was glad to hear her voice. Leslie apologized for disturbing her, but Sandy assured her friend that it was no disturbance at all, she was happy to talk with her. Leslie was wondering if Sandy might be up for some company. She had a free weekend and thought, that if Sandy was agreeable, she would come out to the house on Friday, the day after tomorrow.

"That would be great, Les."

"You're sure? I don't want to bother you."

"Come on, we're friends. Please, it would be wonderful to see you. Besides, you're the lady of the manor, it *is* your house. And I have to admit that I'm getting a little tired of talking to myself."

"Isn't that the only way to have an intelligent conversation? Okay, dear, see you soon," Leslie said.

She eagerly awaited her friend's arrival on Friday. Her anticipation infused her with a jolt of energy and she found herself solving the puzzle of the TotToy page the next day, even though she promised herself that she would never buy a $500 teddy bear for her children, if she ever had any. A plain old Tubby would be good enough.

It was dusk on Friday when Leslie's Jeep Cherokee came bouncing up the road to the house, its headlights cutting through the gloom that had already descended upon the mountain. In her usual exuberant manner, Leslie banged through the front door, her arms full of grocery bags.

"Alms for the poor." She set the bags on the counter in the kitchen. "I thought you might be starving up here." She turned and gave Sandy a hug. "Girl, you look good. I think this fresh air agrees with you."

"You liar," Sandy said, with a smile, running her hand through her disheveled hair. "I've let myself go here in the boonies."

"Hmm, I should let myself go, then, save a few grand on facials and hair treatments."

Leslie talked about herself as if she was an ogre, Sandy thought. That had always been her way, when in fact, she was an attractive woman; petite and slim, with shoulder-length auburn hair.

"Yeah, right," Sandy said. "You crack me up."

They unpacked the groceries. Sandy pulled a bottle of wine out of one of the bags. "Oh, pinot noir, my favorite."

"Of course it is, that's why I brought it."

They chatted in the kitchen while they put together a dinner of salad and grilled chicken. The women had not seen each other in over a month and so, they shared all the gossip and news of their friends that they had heard over that time. After dinner, they took their wine into the living room, killed the first bottle and opened a second as they talked. Sandy was glad the conversation was light, and that Leslie did not mention Kevin, even though she knew her friend was curious. Well, there would be time for that.

The next morning, the women staggered into the kitchen, both feeling the effects of the previous night's drinking.

"I'll die if I don't get some coffee right this very minute," Leslie said, taking a mug from out of the cabinet.

"What happened?" Sandy asked. "We used to be able to drink all night long in college."

"It's called age, dear." Leslie poured hot coffee into her mug. "We need to clear our heads. How about if we take a walk right after breakfast?"

Sandy agreed and shortly after, the women were walking along Dark Entry Road. Although it was summer, the morning was cool and the shade from the deep woods made it cooler. Leslie wore an open flannel shirt, its sleeves rolled up, over a t-shirt, while Sandy wore an old sweatshirt that had belonged to Kevin.

"You know, I've never walked out here before," Sandy said.

"You were only here at the house once before and for a short time."

"That's true." She looked around as they walked, noting how the canopy of trees overhead seemed to form a roof over them. "I've always wondered why more people haven't built houses up here. It seems like prime vacation property."

"We couldn't sell it," Leslie said.

"We?"

Her friend nodded. "My dad owned much of this land—I do now—but he was never able to sell it. Someone would seem interested in buying, but then, for whatever reason, would change their mind. After a while, my dad said, 'the hell with it.' He didn't need the money anyway."

The road was narrow and rutted and they kept to one side, even though it was unlikely that a vehicle would be on it. A path opened on their left and Leslie headed down it. "I want to show you something."

They walked several yards down the path, brambles clutching at their jeans. Leslie stopped before her a stone rectangle roughly ten feet long by eight wide. The moss-covered stones that formed the walls were only about two feet high. In the area enclosed by the walls, the ground was sunken and covered in weedy bushes and a few saplings.

Sandy stepped closer. "What is it?"

"It's a cellar hole. The foundation of an old house. There are a lot of them lying around in the woods if you know where to look. Some old wells, too."

"Who lived here? Do you know?"

"There used to be a village of charcoal burners up here, at least that's what my dad said. The village was founded sometime in the eighteenth-century and lasted for a century or more. They called it Dudleytown."

"What happened to it?"

Leslie shrugged. "I haven't a clue. My dad didn't seem to know either. But he did research a few things about the place. That's how my dad was; if his curiosity was roused by something, he'd try to find out what he could about the subject, usually write it down in one of the many journals he kept. Dad had a million journals going, it seemed."

The women turned and headed back to the road.

"Your father seemed like an interesting man. I wish I had met him," Sandy said.

"He was that, and smart, too."

"It's funny, but I don't recall you talking about him all that much."

They had reached the road again and were slowly walking back toward the house. Leslie was silent. Sandy glanced at her friend.

"Les, are you okay?"

"Yes, it's just hard to talk about him, considering. . ." She stopped and turned to face her friend. "I never told you how he died, I never told anyone."

"No."

"He killed himself, Sandy."

"Oh, god, Les, I'm so sorry." She put her arms around her friend. "That's awful."

Leslie allowed herself to be hugged but stood there like a statue. She continued to talk, and Sandy sensed that she should not interrupt her friend, that Leslie needed to get it all out.

"It was before we met. I was away at school when Ned Buxton, my father's best friend, called me and gave me the news. I couldn't believe it. First, my mother, and then Dad." Tears formed in her eyes. "He had a tough time of it—we both did—when Mom was diagnosed with Alzheimer's disease, but I was away, so I didn't live with it like he did. She was only sixty-four, that's not even old. She deteriorated quickly, a blessing of sorts, I guess. Dad couldn't take care of her anymore, so he put her in a place where she could be taken care of by professionals. It killed him to do that, but he had no choice. She died shortly after."

Leslie wiped away a tear.

"You should have seen the two of them when they were younger. Soul mates in every sense of the word. Dad worshiped her. I guess he just found living without her to be too much for him. Less than two years after she passed away, he shot himself. They found his body in the woods, propped against a tree."

Sandy could imagine him beneath the tree, a bloody hole in his chest, the gun lying in the bushes beside him. The image sent shivers through her.

Leslie took a deep breath and exhaled. She wiped the last of the tears from her eyes. "I'm sorry. I really didn't mean for all that to come out."

Sandy hugged her friend. "That's okay, Les. It seemed like you needed to say it."

She sighed. "Maybe, but maybe some things are better left unspoken."

What had begun as a sunny day took a sudden turn and by mid-afternoon gray clouds scudded over Coltsfoot Mountain. The temperature dropped. Within minutes, fat droplets of rain were splattering on the deck outside.

"We barely missed the rain," Sandy said, from where she stood looking out through the window. Water now streamed down the glass. Beyond the deck, the trees had taken on a deeper color, as though the rain was coating them in a black dye. She rubbed her arms. "It's chilly in here, don't you think?" she said, turning to Leslie.

"Let's have a fire." Leslie rose from where she sat on the couch. "Maybe that's crazy for July, but I agree with you, it's cold in here." There was a stack of firewood on the hearth and she arranged a few logs in the fireplace.

Sandy watched her. "You almost look like you know what you're doing," she said, while her friend used the bellows to pump some air into the fire.

"Girl Scouts never forget how."

"How to do what?" Sandy wiggled her eyebrows at her friend in Groucho Marx style.

Leslie laughed. "We didn't learn that in Girls Scouts."

"Then you probably didn't have much fun."

"Hey, come on. I learned how to knit, bake brownies, take care of a gerbil. . ."

"A gerbil?"

Leslie stood, rubbing her hands together before the fire. "Long story."

"Have you looked outside, lately?" Sandy said, pointing to the water-soaked woods beyond the deck. "We're not going anywhere for a while."

Leslie walked across the room and sat back down on the couch. "There's not much to tell, really. I lost it."

Sandy sat across from her friend. "The gerbil? You lost the gerbil?"

"Somehow it got out of its cage and chewed a hole in the wall. . . "

"Uh-oh."

"Right. It got inside the wall and we couldn't get it out. We could hear it scratching in the wall. We tried knocking on the wall to see if we could scare it back down to the hole, but it wasn't the world's smartest gerbil. My dad tried snaking a coat hanger up the hole to see if he could entice the gerbil out, but that didn't work, either."

"You didn't name this gerbil 'Einstein,' did you?"

"No. Roscoe."

"Really? I didn't see that coming."

"So, anyway, the gerbil never came back. We heard it scratching and running around in the wall, but then, after a few days, we didn't hear it anymore."

"And so now, there's a little gerbil skeleton somewhere in the walls of your old house," Sandy said.

"I guess so."

"Maybe a tiny gerbil ghost as well?"

Leslie laughed. "Who knows? You know, I can laugh about it now, although I still feel guilty, but then . . . it was horrible."

"But they gave you a merit badge anyway?"

"Yes, they did. Maybe it was a consolation prize. But, it wasn't my fault that I had a brain-damaged gerbil."

The women were quiet for a few moments, watching the rain falling outside. The wind had kicked up and now the tree branches flailed in the onslaught, leaves tearing from the limbs and spinning away. But inside, the fire was dancing in the fireplace and the room had warmed up nicely.

"I used to like storms when I was a kid," Leslie said. "It always felt so good to watch them from the safety of a nice warm house."

"What about now?"

"Yes, this is nice."

"Let's make it nicer." She got up and went into the kitchen. Leslie heard her rummaging around in the cabinet. She returned with an open bottle of wine and two glasses. She filled the glasses and handed one to her friend. "Here's to scary storms and safe houses." They clinked glasses and drank.

"You seem to be in a good mood, Sandy."

"I guess I am. It has been peaceful here and I'm getting some work done."

"And Kevin?" There, she had said it, even though she had told herself that she would wait until Sandy brought the subject up herself.

"Yes, I've been thinking about him, of course." She set her glass on the table and leaned forward on the couch. "But it's odd that I haven't felt the pain that I thought I would. I've cried, oh yes, I've cried, but I feel now that I'm cried out, that there's nothing more to cry about. Does that make sense?"

"I think so. Maybe you're getting a dose of reality?"

"Could be, Les. In my rational moments, I know that a future with him is impossible. Maybe now, I'm having only rational moments."

"Have you spoken with him?"

Sandy shook her head. "No, although I'll admit it, I've been tempted to call him. But, he hasn't called or emailed me, either. It's been a few days now and it's like he doesn't even care that I'm gone."

"Bingo."

"And I know that if he called you to try and find me that you would tell me."

"Of course. He hasn't, by the way."

"I know." She picked up her glass and took a sip. She held the wine in her mouth a few seconds, savoring it, before swallowing. "Les, I was wondering, do you need me to be out of here anytime soon?"

"From the house? No, sweetie, you can stay as long as want."

"I'm not saying that I will stay much longer, I don't know, it would just be good to know that I have a place if I need it."

"For as long as you want, Sandy."

The two friends drank their wine and talked about anything and everything while the fire popped and crackled on the hearth.

Outside, dusk and fog spread over the house, plunging the woods into a surreal darkness that was night, but not quite night. The rain was beginning to taper off. Other than the trees swaying and creaking in the wind, nothing else moved in the woods. While all the woodland creatures seemed to be snuggled up somewhere, waiting out the storm, one pair of eyes peered through the fading light, watching the house and the two women inside.

FIVE

Rain sluiced through his hair, dripping into his face, but it didn't bother him. He was accustomed to being out in the elements. Besides, he was too busy watching Lady and Yellow Lady to pay any mind to the weather. It was not easy to see the women through the rain and fog, so he crept closer to the house. The lights inside gave him a much better view.

He could see them sitting inside, talking. He guessed that their voices were pretty, like birds. He wished he could hear them. Maybe he should go inside. There was a way in. They would never know.

As he was giving that idea some thought, Yellow Lady got up and came to the window. She stood there looking out, looking directly at him where he stood enshrouded in the bushes. She looked right at him, not more than fifteen feet away. He stood completely still, his heart thumping. All he could do was stare back at her.

He was certain that she had detected him, but no, Yellow Lady hadn't seen him. She remained at the window calmly watching the rain. His heart slowed and now, he knew he could look at her safely. The last time he had seen her was when she was on the deck, but he was not as close to her then as he was now. Yellow Lady was magic, he thought, beautiful magic. She wore jeans and a blue sweatshirt that seemed too big for her. Her long blonde hair was pulled back and tied into a long tail. He wondered what it would feel like to touch her hair, to touch her face. He thought she would like that.

He felt those strange stirrings again deep inside him as he watched her. They were pleasurable, but in an odd way, almost painful. They seemed full of memory and made him think of things unseen, things once in the hand but now lost. What were those things? They seemed to taunt him from the edge of his memory, but they would not be dragged into the daylight. A shiver coursed through him that had nothing to do with the cold rain.

Suddenly, Yellow Lady turned and walked back to the couch. She said something to Lady and Lady laughed. He could not hear them, but he smiled as well because Yellow Lady was talking to him, too, even if she didn't know it.

Lady held a glass in her hand. He watched her drink and noticed the whiteness of her throat, like a deer's belly. Lady was pretty, too, although he did not think she was magic like Yellow Lady.

From his hiding place in the bushes, he continued to watch the two women. The rain finally abated and Yellow Lady got up and walked deeper into the house where he could no longer see her. Lady also rose from the couch and turned off the light. The room went dark. He remained hidden and was about to leave when a light came on from above. There was a loft up there and when he looked up, he saw light illuminating the exposed rafters of the ceiling. From his vantage point that was all he could see, so he slipped out of the bushes, about to return to the woods.

A second light came on at ground level, casting a dim square of white across the clearing.

He stole around to the side of the house and found the lighted window. Carefully, he inched closer. Curtains were partly drawn across the window. He saw a shadow moving behind them. Slowly, he moved closer to the window until his hands were on the sill. He noticed a gap in the curtains and moved closer to the window. It was higher than he was tall, but there was a rock below the window upon which he could stand. Finally, he was able to peer in through the curtains.

Lady was in the room. A single lamp on a small table beside a bed provided soft light in the room. She sat on the bed wearing a red t-shirt and jeans. The flannel shirt she had been wearing earlier lay across the bed. She was leafing through a small spiral-bound notebook, pausing every now and then to read. Sometimes, she smiled. Sometimes, it seemed she was crying. It made him sad to see her cry. He could just see the top of a box that stood on the floor near the bed. It seemed to be filled with more notebooks.

He wondered what Lady was doing, what it was that made her smile and cry at the same time. After a few minutes, she closed the notebook and placed it back in the box. She bent over, and he thought that she must be sliding the box under the bed.

Lady walked out of his sight and when she returned, she was wearing a nightgown. She climbed into bed and turned out the light.

He remained there, his face pressed against the glass, the image of her reading her book still etched upon his mind. He wondered if Lady would like him to visit her now. That would be nice, he thought, but then, he remembered her crying and thought, no, not yet.

Reluctantly, he withdrew from the window and made his way across the clearing into the woods. His feet remembered the way back to his shack in the ravine and it was a good thing they did since his thoughts were entirely taken up by the women at the house. He came across the old cellar hole just at the head of the ravine. Working his way behind it, he found the ravine, well hidden in dense undergrowth and nimbly made his way down it, despite the mud and rain-slicked stones. He reached the bottom and walked a few more yards until he came to the scrap-lumber shack nestled in an indentation in the steep side of the ravine.

He slid aside the piece of weathered plywood that served as a door and ducked inside the shack. Despite its ramshackle appearance, the shack was dry. The old stained mattress upon which he collapsed was damp with humidity, but not wet. The three walls built into the ravine were riddled with gaps, but the shack's location deep within the defile kept out the wind and rain. The rear wall of the shack was the side of the ravine itself. An old blanket pinned up against it kept out dirt and mud. In the center of that natural wall stood a rectangular white stone. The face of the stone was smooth and level. There were letters carved into it. His reading skills were rudimentary, at best, so he never paid much attention to them. They were a mystery. Mostly worn away, the ciphers that remained read: *Q . . . nt . . . Rand . . . 1868.*

He flopped on the mattress and tried to sleep, but his mind filled with images that made him restless and kept him awake. When he finally fell asleep, he dreamed and in those dreams, he saw the women and they called to him. *Come to us*, they said.

When Kevin finally awoke, he found the blanket on the bed beside him thrown back. Maria had already left the apartment. She didn't leave a note, but that didn't surprise him either. What could she say? He had felt something in the air between them ever since they had met at that Dr. Pepper shoot, but he did not see her that often and when he did, it was always on business. That he should happen to run into her at Louie's Place was simply coincidence. What happened later seemed inevitable, considering Maria's complaints about her boring husband who was always away from home on business, and her taste for coke.

He rubbed his eyes and sat up in bed. The room was filled with light. The clock beside the bed read 10:30. Next to the clock was a compact mirror and a razor blade, incriminating evidence of last night's little binge. There were still a few tiny grains of white powder on the mirror, so he licked a fingertip, pressed it to the powder and held his finger up to his nose inhaling the powder. Probably not much there to do any good, he thought, but why waste it?

He pulled back the blanket and swung his legs over the side of the bed. He was naked and the sunlight entering the room warmed his body. He thought of Maria. How such a hot little Latina could get stuck with a buttoned-down nerd of a husband was beyond him, but that was her problem. He was happy enough to give her a night that she needed—and it was obvious that she *really* needed it—but that was all. He didn't expect to hear from her, nor did he have any illusions about what last night meant to him. It was recreational sex, pure and simple. Not that he would refuse her, should they happen to find themselves in a similar circumstance in the future, but there would be no strings, he was certain of that. He thought that Maria probably felt the same way.

He got up and walked into the bathroom. After a quick shower, he dressed and sat down for a breakfast of coffee and a toasted bagel. Sounds of the city floated up to the tenth-floor apartment, but he was accustomed to them and paid them little notice. He sipped his coffee and, last night's romp already a memory, thought about Sandy. Four days had passed since she had left. She hadn't called him, and he would not call her, not yet anyway. After all, she had walked out on him. She knew where to find him when she wanted to come back. And she would come back, he was sure.

Still, he did miss her. She always made quite an impression whenever they went out. He noticed how heads turned in her direction when she walked by and he could read the other men's minds: *lucky bastard,* they said. Yes, Sandy was quite the prize. In the two years that they had been together he had been more or less faithful to her, but their very longevity—more than he had ever given to any other woman—was proof, he thought, of his feelings for her.

He spread a little cream cheese on a second bagel. What did she have to complain about? Okay, sure, that little slap he had given her was out of line, but he had apologized for it. Why wasn't that good enough for her? He wasn't the kind of guy that went around hitting women, it was just that she had really pushed his buttons that time. It was a knee-jerk reaction, a one-time thing. Why couldn't she see that? Why couldn't she just let it go?

His cell phone buzzed, and he grabbed it. Speaking of the devil, he thought, but no, the screen read *Butthead,* the name he called his best friend Roger.

"Morning, Butthead."

"Fuck you too, Shit-for-Brains. What's up?" Roger said.

"Just having my breakfast."

"Hey, I want to remind you that I'll swing by tomorrow at noon, so we can go to the game."

Kevin had forgotten that they had tickets for the Yankees game, but that would be a nice diversion. "Yeah, that's cool."

"Sandy will let you go, right?"

"Number one, Butthead, she's away visiting a friend," Kevin lied, "and two, I do what I want, when I want. She doesn't own me."

"She doesn't? Shit, she can own me anytime she wants."

"You are a butthead, aren't you?" he said, with a laugh.

"Gotta love me," Roger said. "Tomorrow, homes."

He sat at the table, looking at his cell phone. He picked it up and scrolled through the messages one more time, just to make sure. There was no message from her. He deleted all the messages and slid the phone into his pants pocket.

Where had she gone? It was unlikely that she had gone to her mother's house in Jersey. With their estranged relationship, it would be a cold day in Hell before she sought comfort there. Leslie probably knew, but Kevin also knew that she wouldn't tell him. Leslie was not a big fan of his, he was aware of that, but he didn't care for her all that much, either. He remembered Sandy talking about a place that Leslie's father owned in Connecticut. Was it in Kent? Could she have gone there with Leslie? He supposed that was possible, but in any case, he was in no mood to go chasing after her, no matter where she had gone. Not yet, maybe never.

He thought he'd head down to the studio and do some work. It was Saturday, but that didn't make any difference to him. When you are self-employed, you work when you work, which seemed to be almost all the time. He looked around the apartment, maybe expecting to see Sandy suddenly materialize there like a ghost, then walked out, locking the door behind him.

SIX

Sandy waved as Leslie backed her Cherokee out of the driveway. Monday, and Leslie was due back at work. Sandy stood on the front step watching her friend bump down Dark Entry Road. She smiled. It had been nice having her there for the weekend. It had been like an extended sleep-over and it had been way too long since they had shared so much time together.

The storm that had drowned the mountain in rain had passed by and now, golden bars of sunshine filtered down through the trees. She stood there for a moment more, breathing in the fresh air. The scent of honeysuckle tickled her senses. The woods crowding around the house were still and quiet. Once again, she noticed the absence of birds or even the sound of birdsong. That seemed odd.

She stepped inside the house and closed the door.

She went upstairs to the loft and sat on the bed. She checked her email on the laptop and found nothing of interest, other than a message from Paul, her contact at the TotToy Company, asking for an update on their Web site's progress. She had half-hoped that there would be a message from Kevin, "half-hoped" because she would like to think that he was looking for her, wanting to speak with her, but then, she was not sure what she would say, or even if she truly wanted to respond to him. She sighed. What to do?

She and Leslie had talked about him. Leslie did not care for him, no, didn't like him, but she was too good a friend to let that affect their friendship. Still, as close as they were, Sandy could not bring herself to mention the fact that he had hit her. Leslie would demand that she file a police report, something that Sandy would never do. The whole incident was simply too embarrassing to talk about. It's not as though he had beaten her, after all. Everybody loses their temper once in a while. Perhaps, she had brought about his outburst herself. She had been badgering him about what she saw as his cocaine addiction—which he would deny. Shouldn't he know if he had an addiction? She could understand his anger if, maybe, she had pushed him a little too far. Kevin was a proud man and he did not take criticism well.

She tried to do some work, but she found that she was unable to concentrate, even with the five-hundred-dollar teddy bear sitting by the laptop for inspiration. Maybe if she put her work—and thoughts of Kevin—aside for a little bit, she could clear her mind and come back to it later, at least the work part.

She thought a walk might be just the thing. She had noticed on her walk with Leslie that there were several trails meandering through the woods. It might be fun to explore some of them. She slipped her cell phone into her pocket, laced up her Reeboks, and left the house, dropping the key into her pocket.

She walked down Dark Entry Road. It really was not much of a road. Narrow, rutted, mostly gravel, and dotted with patches of grass and weeds, it was more an insane engineer's idea of a road, than an actual thoroughfare. Considering, though, that Leslie's house was the only one on the mountain and that the road was so little traveled, it was amazing it existed at all. The woods had not yet reclaimed it. Since she had been at the house, Sandy had not seen or heard another car on the road, other than Leslie's Cherokee. Here and there, on either side of the road, fragments of old stone walls—ubiquitous in Connecticut—sank into the earth like old tombstones. Draped in lichen and moss, they were nearly indistinguishable from the surrounding woods.

Suddenly, a small animal darted across the road before her. It was a chipmunk, its tail raised like an antenna. It stopped for a moment atop a rock, shot her a glance, and then disappeared into the bushes. The little beast had startled her, and she realized that was because she simply had not seen much of any wildlife here on the mountain, a place in which one would expect just the opposite.

She found the same narrow path that she and Leslie had taken on their walk. She walked down it and came to the cellar hole. The arrangement of stones appealed to her sense of design and she took out her cell phone and used its camera to take a few pictures. Sandy noticed that the path continued down behind the hole. She followed it. After a few yards, she discovered a small circle of stones just off the path. A thick mat of leaves, twigs, and stones lay within the perimeter about two feet below the surface. An inch or so of the previous day's rain lay upon the debris. She guessed that the hole was probably the remains of an old well that had serviced the house that used to be there.

She followed the path around a bend and down a ridge. After another thirty yards or so, the path broadened. She discovered another cellar hole. Unlike the first one, this hole was mostly clear of vegetation. Many of the stones that had been a part of the foundation of the house had toppled into the hole, but there was little in the hole other than the stones. She snapped a few more pictures.

As she looked through the viewscreen, she noticed something parchment-colored lying among the stones. She put the phone back into her pocket and moved closer to the edge, trying to identify the object. She couldn't tell what it was, but it didn't seem to belong there. Curious, she gingerly made her way over the wall and down into the hole.

From beneath the rocks she pulled out the broken half of a dirty Ouija board. What the hell? She remembered playing with the mysterious Ouija board when she was a child, she and her girlfriends asking the board about future boyfriends and husbands and giggling over the board's answers. A child's game. What was such a game doing here? Who had used it?

She dug around in the rocks but did not find the other half of the board, but she did find the melted stubs of two red candles. Weird.

A chill came over her, as though a cloud had suddenly passed before the sun. She left the board and the candles in the hole, but took a picture of them lying there, and then climbed out of the hole.

She quickened her pace as she retraced her steps back home feeling just like a scared kid, as though someone was following her. Of course, that was impossible.

She fumbled with the key in the lock. Once again, she had the uneasy feeling that someone was following her. She turned to look over her shoulder just as the door opened, but saw nothing, a breeze perhaps, shivering the leaves of the bushes across the road, but nothing more. She went inside and closed the door firmly behind her, breathing a sigh of relief, but feeling silly about it at the same time. What had made her nervous? There was nothing out there.

She bent down to untie her sneakers—she hated to wear shoes inside—and that's when she spotted the leaf. A single green leaf lay on the wood floor only a few feet from the door. She didn't remember seeing it as she had left the house. Sandy picked it up and examined it as if it held some clue about how it had materialized there. Could she have tracked it inside on her shoes? No, it was too far from the door. She hadn't stepped there. It must have blown in when she opened the door. She simply hadn't noticed it until now. She kicked off her sneakers and dropped the leaf in the garbage in the kitchen.

Sandy was not a nervous woman, but that leaf nagged her, so she made a quick inspection of the house, beginning with the loft and then, coming back downstairs. Nothing amiss so far, just as she had expected. She came to Leslie's room on the ground floor and stood in the doorway. Everything looked alright there, too, although she noticed a carton half pulled out from under the bed. That wasn't like Leslie, she thought. That woman was a neat freak. It seemed out of character for her to leave the carton lying there like that. Maybe she had simply forgotten it was there.

She entered the room. The carton did not have a top and she saw that it was filled with spiral notebooks in assorted sizes and colors. The contents of the box were really none of her business, she thought, but her curiosity got the better of her and she took out one of the notebooks. It was a medium-sized red notebook with *2008* written on the cover. She sat on Leslie's bed and flipped open the book. She knew her friend's hand and the handwriting that covered the lined pages of the book was not Leslie's. The letters were scrawled more than they were written, and she had the impression that the writer was masculine. Her suspicions were confirmed when she started to read one of the dated entries in what was clearly a journal. The author was Ted O'Neil, Leslie's father. Once Sandy realized that she was reading the man's personal journal, she closed it and put it back in the carton. She had no right to be reading it.

But she remembered Leslie saying that her father was a perpetual journal keeper and that he had journals for everything. Maybe there was something in the carton that would be of interest, but that would not be of a personal nature, something she was sure Leslie would not mind her reading. She sorted through the various notebooks, reading the titles written on their covers. Besides several notebooks titled with single years, there were others with succinct titles: *Politics*, *Sports*, *Travel U.S.*, *Travels Abroad*, and others. She stopped when she came to a blue notebook titled *Dudleytown*. Leslie had said that was the name of the community of charcoal burners that had lived on the mountain long ago. This could be interesting. She pulled the notebook out of the carton, sure that Leslie would not mind. She slid the box with the remaining journals back under the bed.

Her nervousness about the leaf was completely forgotten as she walked out of the bedroom, flipping through the pages of the notebook. It seemed that Ted O' Neil had a lot to say about Dudleytown. He had almost filled the book with his writing. She slid open the glass door to the deck and settled on the *chaise* with the notebook.

None of the entries in the Dudleytown journal were dated, although many of them had titles, and they were thrown together in a disorganized fashion, as though Ted O'Neil simply wrote a new section whenever he uncovered some new information. With some of the entries, though, O'Neil at least cited the sources of the information, most of it coming from various books in the possession of the Cornwall Historical Society.

On the first page of the notebook was a crude map of Dudleytown drawn in black and red ink. Geographic features, such as Coltsfoot Mountain and the adjacent Bald Mountain and Dudleytown Hill were also lined out in black, as was Bonney Brook and Spruce Swamp. It was easy to see how the three elevations threw a perpetual shadow over the abandoned town. The black ink marked the two roads that ran through Dudleytown—Dark Entry Road and Cook Road. Red ink spots along the roads marked the locations of houses, with the name of the owners printed beside them. O'Neil had written below the map an explanation that the house sites spanned the time period 1747-1920. There was also a red star marking the location of the O'Neil house on Dark Entry Road.

She studied the map, surprised by how few houses were listed on it, no more than two dozen or so. Dudleytown was never much of a town, it seemed. She was also surprised to see two schools listed on the map, but no churches or meeting houses, no stores, not even a cemetery. What kind of place was this?

She riffled through the pages. A page titled "The Curse" caught her eye. What curse? She began to read and was soon transfixed by what Leslie's father had recorded there. According to him, Dudleytown took its name from the three Dudley brothers—Abiel, Barzallai, and Gideon—that settled on the land between 1748 and 1754. Other families also moved up the mountains at the same time. It seems that the Dudley family was saddled with a curse that went back a few centuries. In 1510, in merry old England, Edmund Dudley lost his head for plotting to overthrow the English king. Edmund's son John tried to place his own son Guilford on the throne by marrying him to Lady Jane Grey. That plot failed and all three of them wound up placing their heads on the executioner's chopping block. John Dudley had another son that died of the plague and yet another, Robert, who was smart enough to leave England forever. His son William came to America in 1630 and it was his sons who eventually settled in the little village that soon bore their name.

What a story, she thought. It would make a great reality TV show—*Those Damned Dudleys*.

But the story of the curse didn't end there.

What followed was an incredible litany of tragedies and mishaps, insanity and murder, that plagued the villagers from the time the Dudleys settled there, right up until 1930, when a doctor who owned a summer home in the village returned there to his wife after a few days in New York City, only to find her cowering in an upstairs bedroom, cackling and muttering to herself, completely insane.

She read about how Abiel Dudley went insane and became a pauper and how, almost a century later, a man named Brophy also went mad, ranting about demons and strange entities with hoofed feet. In 1764, most of the Carter family was massacred by Indians, three of their children taken into captivity, while two cholera epidemics took many of the villagers. In 1792 the body of Gershon Hollister was found murdered in William Tanner's house and, although Tanner was acquitted of the crime, he too went insane, grumbling about demons. A woman was struck and killed by lightning in 1804 as she stood on her front porch and Mary Cheney, the wife of Horace Greeley, put a rope around her neck and stepped off a chair.

There was even more, but she could not read any further. She closed the notebook. Could all those horrible things really have happened here? Ted O'Neil had written a brief note at the end expressing his doubts about all those accounts being true, saying that he hoped to do more research about them.

Had he done that? What had he discovered?

SEVEN

Insanity. The people of Dudleytown had been plagued by madness driving them to murder and suicide, leaving some of them babbling idiots, muttering to themselves as they wandered aimlessly through the village. Horrible. But what could have caused such an outbreak of lunacy, a malignant disease that lasted for almost two centuries? The curse of the Dudleys?

Sandy set the notebook on her lap and gazed into the deep woods beyond the clearing. Nothing but darkness there. Even at high noon on the brightest day, the woods were gloomy, a preternatural haze like dusk filling the air. These woods were like the deep, dark woods of fairy tales, inhabited by witches and trolls, elves and monsters. Even Little Red Riding Hood would pause to reconsider before venturing down their paths. She recalled the Ouija board and the candles and felt a shiver pass through her. They seemed ritualistic, menacing.

In their stillness, the woods were mesmerizing. Perhaps it was the woods themselves that drove people to madness. Some force, some power that called to them from the darkness, urging them on to unspeakable acts, such as suicide. A thought came to her then, something she had known but forgotten in the moment of discovering the notebooks. Ted O'Neil had killed himself, too. Jesus! Right here in these woods, he had used a shotgun to blow a hole in his chest.

Was it still here? Whatever had created the madness, did it still lurk in the dark woods?

She felt sick to her stomach, as though she had just discovered that bloody body propped against the tree, the gaping red hole blooming in its chest like a grotesque rose. She closed her eyes as though that would shut out the macabre vision, but it did not and instead, as if in a nightmare, she saw the eyes of the corpse fly open and stare in horror, not at her, but at something behind her, something she dared not turn to see.

She opened her eyes and started from the *chaise*, knocking the notebook to the deck, as a man suddenly came around the corner of the house. He was equally as startled to see her on the deck.

"Oh, sorry," he said. "I didn't mean to scare you."

But she was scared. She leaped to her feet, her cell phone in hand. "Who are you? I can call '911' in a second, you know."

The man smiled but kept his distance. He put his hands up as though she pointed a gun at him. "That's not necessary. But if you want to call someone, call Leslie, she'll vouch for me. I do some work for her around the house."

She eyed him suspiciously. He seemed to be about her age and had brown hair and hazel eyes. He was neatly dressed in khaki-colored pants and a denim work shirt. He didn't really look like a bad guy—in fact, he was attractive—but she lived in New York City and knew there was no such thing as looking like a bad guy; they came in all stripes. Just think Ted Bundy.

"Work, huh? What's your name?"

"Nathan Bishop," the man said. "Go ahead, call Leslie. I'll stay right here."

Keeping an eye on the man, she called Leslie and when she answered, asked her friend about him.

"Oh, sweetie, I'm so sorry," Leslie said, "I completely forgot to tell you about him. Yes, Nathan does look after the house. Sometimes, I have chores for him to do, other times he just comes up on his own and does whatever needs to be done. He's a dear. He used to help out my dad as well."

"Describe him to me, Les." She kept an eye on the man who stood just beyond the deck, a bemused smile upon his face.

"He's a hunk." Sandy laughed aloud, despite her attempt to maintain a serious demeanor.

"Les . . ." she whispered, into the phone.

"Sorry, but he is. Okay, then." She went on to describe a man that matched the man who stood with his hands in his pockets, looking at Sandy.

"Fine, Les, that's him. By the way, no more surprises, okay?"

"Got it. Sorry."

She slid her phone into her pocket. "Les says you're alright," she called to Nathan.

"Alright? That's not exactly a ringing endorsement," he said. "Again, my apologies. I saw the car out front, but when no one answered my knock on the front door, I thought I'd check around back. And there you were."

She relaxed. Leslie spoke well of him and he did seem nice enough. "Sorry I went cop on you."

"No, not at all," he said, with a wave of his hand. "This is the only house up here." He looked around at the woods behind him. "And it can get a little creepy in these woods."

She took a few steps across the deck and leaned against the rail. "Leslie said you do odd jobs for her. What brought you out today?"

"That last rainstorm." He looked around again, a movement that made her wonder if he was looking for something. "With all that wind and all, I thought I should check and make sure that no tree limbs came down on the house. It looks like you survived, though," he said, with a smile.

"Yes, I guess we did."

He nodded. "Do you mind my asking your name?"

"Sandy Lawrence."

"Nice to meet you, Sandy Lawrence. Will you be staying up here for a while?"

She shrugged. "Don't know, maybe, maybe not."

"Okay. You know, if there's anything I can do for you while you're here, just let me know." He reached for his wallet and took out a business card. He passed it up to her where she stood on the deck. He held the card in his left hand and she noticed that he did not wear a wedding ring.

"Thank you. I'm sure I'll be fine."

"Of course, but if you need groceries, firewood, whatever, just let me know. I'm out and about a lot. Maybe I'll swing by occasionally—if that's okay with you—just to check in on you."

He seemed sincere and Leslie trusted him completely. She thought she had nothing to fear from him and maybe a little company now and then might be a nice thing.

"Yes, that would be okay."

The ravine was buried in shadow beneath the dense woods and it was dark as night inside the shack. A candle stuck in a tin can glowed on the crate that served as a table. The candlelight sent strange shadows flitting like bats across the walls. The smooth stone in the back of the shack reflected pearly-white in the flickering light.

He sat on the old mattress, staring intently at the candle, watching something moving within its flame. Fire mesmerized him. The twisting, sinuous flame, the dancing spirits inside it, the other spirits cast out as shadows flying around the room. There was magic in fire, and prophecy as well if one knew how to read it.

There was a message for him in the candle's halo and what he read there filled him with dread. Not again, he thought, please, not again. But the spirit in the flame could not be denied. It was the messenger and it was always truthful. His hands trembled, and he closed his eyes, trying to shut out the vision he saw growing in the flame, but even with his eyes closed, the vision remained imprinted in his mind, a vision he had seen before. A chill shivered his spine.

He opened his eyes.

He heard the hooting of an owl outside, a sound to which he had once been well accustomed, but which he had not he heard for a long time. They were returning. He had come to understand the mournful language of the owls and what they told him now only increased his fear. They, too, knew of the vision.

The spirit within the flame was persistent and demanded his attention. His eyes were once again drawn to the light. He was powerless to turn away. He crouched by the candle, clutching his knees to his chest.

Inside the blue heart of the flame, he saw it, a tiny dancing figure, the same dancing figure he had seen before, the same figure that unleashed a horror upon the mountain which plagued his dreams for so many sleepless nights. He did not know why he had been spared that last time when the horror stalked the woods, but he had.

He was the only one that escaped.

But now, the spirit in the flame warned him of the impending horror. The sachem was coming. Again.

Scooting back against the white stone, he hugged his knees, rocking gently just as he remembered being rocked so long ago; when? He heard the owls flitting through the woods. In his mind's eye, he could see the tiny dancing figure in the flame growing larger. He could see it taking shape deep within the woods, could sense its presence growing everywhere around him like the wind.

The last time, he had not understood the message in the flame. He could tell that the owls were agitated, but he did not know why, nor did he connect their strange behavior with the events that later unfolded, at least, not until it was too late. But he did have the feeling something strange was happening on the mountain. The deer carcass, for example. It was not unusual for him to find the bodies of dead animals from time to time as he wandered the woods and there would have been nothing out of the ordinary in finding the deer carcass, except for the way it apparently died, its entire hindquarters ripped from the rest of the body and discarded several feet away. The entrails had been dragged through the bushes and were partially eaten by other animals.

He stood there looking at the carcass. He could not see any puncture wounds, either from bullets or arrows, so the animal had not been killed by hunters. Other than the fact that the animal had been torn in two, there were no other marks of struggle on its body. The glassy eyes of the deer, now covered by flies, yielded no clue as to how the animal had met its death.

Coyotes? There were a few coyotes on the mountain, but they were incapable of such a kill. Wolves? There hadn't been any reports of wolves in the area for over a century, maybe longer.

He circled the carcass, both mystified and frightened. Whatever had ripped the deer apart had incredible strength, superhuman strength. And it was on his mountain.

He kept close to his shack after that, afraid to venture out into the woods where he might meet up with the monstrous thing that had slaughtered the deer. One night, while settled safely within his shack, a loud shriek split the night, causing him to spring up from the mattress, trembling. He stood there in the darkness, his ears straining for every little sound, but the woods had gone instantly silent—no shriek, no owls, nothing. It was not a warm night, but he felt sweat trickle down his brow as he stood there still as death, afraid to move, afraid to breathe. How long he stood there like that he didn't know. After what seemed like a long time, he heard an owl give a tentative hoot. It was followed moments later by another and soon the owls were back

Whatever creature had made that ghastly sound was gone now. He could feel the woods return to their normal rhythm. Gradually, he recovered from his fear and went back to sleep, but not before moving the crate up against the plywood door to give him one more layer of protection, flimsy as it might be, from whatever was out there.

Those two events should have prepared him for what came later, but they did not.

And now, the sachem was back.

He rocked himself on the mattress, singing quietly a song she—the witch?—had taught him so long ago, trying to calm his frazzled nerves. He glanced at the candle and, even from that distance, saw the figure, the sachem, dancing inside.

He had seen the sachem only once. A misty figure, slipping through the trees. Faintly luminous, it was shot through with tiny sparkles like fireflies. It had its back to him and was moving quickly away without so much as disturbing a single leaf. After that, he did not leave his shack for four days.

EIGHT

Enough is enough, Kevin thought. It had already been four days and he had not heard anything from Sandy. What the hell was wrong with her? It wasn't so much that he worried about her, but people were starting to talk. His friends were asking why they hadn't seen her lately and he didn't like the suspicion he saw in their eyes. He knew what they were thinking, but nobody walked out on Kevin Perillo, they must know that. He was always the walker.

It was time she was back where she belonged. They could talk it out if that's what she wanted, maybe come to some kind of understanding. He wasn't an unreasonable man. As long as she understood a few things about him that he just wasn't about to change for her, or for any woman, everything would be fine.

He was certain he would never hit her again. He admitted he had lost control—although he still thought she had been too pushy—and he promised himself never to resort to violence again, no matter the circumstances. He was not that kind of guy.

He could call her, but he knew she would not take his call. If she wanted to talk with him she would already have called him. Maybe he should go to her, surprise her, and then she would have to talk to him. That's probably what she wanted, anyway, for him to come to her, to convince her to go back to New York with him where everything would turn out just fine. She was probably just waiting for him to do that. Crawl to her.

He wasn't the type to beg. No way. But he thought that, in a sense, she was playing a game with him. No doubt, she wanted to come back to him, but he had wounded her pride. He had his pride, too, as the skeptical expression on his friends' faces reminded him, but perhaps he could set it aside, just this once. He could imagine himself walking into *Theresa's* arm in arm with Sandy, heads turning and people whispering, *That Kevin, what a lucky bastard.*

So, okay, he would go to her and bring her back to New York. But he had to find her first. He guessed Leslie probably knew where she was, but he also knew the bitch would not tell him a fucking thing. He'd play detective. He'd find her.

He knew Leslie's vacation house was somewhere in Connecticut, not too far over the New York border. It wasn't on the Gold Coast, among the estates of the wealthy on the shore. No, the house was further inland. The large road atlas he pulled out from under a pile of photography magazines beneath the coffee table was old and dog-eared, but so was Connecticut he thought, with a laugh. He'd find the town. Looking at the map, the logical area to find her would be somewhere along Route 7. He seemed to remember her talking about that road. He ran his finger over the route, scanning the names of the towns along the way. Danbury, New Milford, Kent, Kent Furnace—an odd name, he thought. A bridge. He remembered Leslie saying something about a bridge. He found two—Bull's Bridge and Cornwall Bridge. Worth the shot, he thought.

He threw some clothes in an overnight bag, locked the apartment, and hit the road. The black Camaro he gunned down the highway, now that he had left the city behind, was only a few months old. With the air-conditioning on and the music cranked up, he was in high spirits. The Camaro's engine roared. He was having an adventure.

He turned north onto Route 7 from the Merritt Parkway. Once he was above Danbury, the scenery turned absolutely bucolic, interrupted now and then by small towns. A few cows. A little sign announcing Bulls' Bridge came into view and he slowed the car, thinking that was one of the towns in which he might find her.

Only there was no town. Bull's Bridge Road crossed Route 7 and off to his left he could see where that road entered an old covered bridge spanning the Housatonic River, but that was all there was to Bull's Bridge, a bridge. Scratch one.

He had better luck as he drove further north and came to Cornwall. Another covered bridge, painted red, came into view and just beyond it, Kevin saw a town. He turned off the road and slowed down as he entered the narrow old bridge. Even at a slow speed the engine sounds echoed loudly off the wooden walls and trusses of the bridge. Emerging into the sunlight once again, he found a service station on the other side and turned into it.

He got out of the car and went inside. The kid sitting there with his feet up on a chair said, "Awesome car, man," when Kevin entered. Reluctantly, he stood up and stepped behind the register on the counter.

"Thanks. Give me twenty bucks premium," Kevin said, pulling a bill out of his wallet. He watched as the kid rang him up. "I'm looking for a house here. Do you know a person named Leslie O'Neil?"

"O'Neil? Yeah, everyone knows the O'Neil's. Well, I mean, the old man's dead now, but his daughter still comes back now and then. Why?" the kid asked, his mood suddenly turned wary.

Had he said something wrong to the kid? He couldn't imagine what that would have been. "I'm just looking for the O'Neil house. A friend of mine is a friend of Leslie's and she invited me up."

"To the house?"

"No, to the Vatican." Was this kid just a bit slow? "Yes," he said, "to the house."

"Huh. Well, you passed it. Go on back down seven, not far at all, just a little ways. You'll see a road on your left, but look closely, it's easy to miss. It's called Dark Entry Road. You'll probably see a No Trespassing sign, too."

"No trespassing?"

"Yeah, they keep posting that sign, but someone always comes along and takes it down."

Now Kevin was sure the kid was slow. What the fuck was he talking about? "So, the house is on Dark Entry Road?" The kid nodded. "How will I know which one it is?"

The kid laughed. "Don't worry about that, man. It's the only house up there."

Well, that was quick, Sandy thought, as she saw Nathan Bishop's white pick-up truck pull up beside the house the very next day. She went to the front door and opened it, stepping out onto the porch. Nathan was already out of the truck, retrieving something from the bed. He was wearing shorts and she found herself looking too long at the muscles in his tanned calves. He looked up and smiled at her.

"Sorry," he said, as he lifted a carton out of the back of the truck. "I really don't mean to bother you, but my garden's been growing like crazy and I thought that maybe you might like some fresh vegetables." He stood there holding the carton expectantly, like a dog waiting for a treat after fetching his master's newspaper.

She stifled a laugh. "Vegetables?"

"Yes," he said, walking up to the porch. "Nothing fancy, I don't have a lot of time for gardening, but I've got the basics here. Tomatoes, peppers, radishes, some other stuff. I just thought you might be able to use them."

"That's nice of you," she said. "Here, I'll take them."

"I'll bring them inside for you," he said.

She stepped aside, letting him carry the carton into the kitchen, where he set it upon the counter. She noticed that his arms were as well-toned and tanned as his legs. She peered into the box. There were enough vegetables in there to last her for a week or more.

"Thank you."

"No problem," he said, turning to her.

She noticed a fine sheen of perspiration upon his brow. "It's hot. Would you like something to drink?"

"That'd be great. Iced tea, if you've got it."

She had a pitcher of tea in the refrigerator and poured two glasses for them. They sat at the kitchen table. They sat there in silence for a few moments, sipping on the tea. She watched him and noticed how his hazel eyes scanned the room and the window to the woods beyond, as though he was looking for something. He did it surreptitiously, so as not to draw attention to his actions, but she noticed them anyway. Then, he turned his attention to her.

"So, how are you making out here?"

She detected a serious tone in his voice that struck her as odd, especially since she had just seen him yesterday. "I'm fine."

He nodded and glanced out the window once again.

"Are you looking for something?"

"Oh, no, not really," he said, both hands wrapped around the glass sitting on the table. He leaned back in the chair. "Did you know Ted O'Neil?"

"No, I didn't. Why?"

"He was a great guy. I did a lot of work for him, but truth be told, I just liked to come up and visit with him." He took a drink from his glass.

"Leslie's told me about him," she said. "I've read some of his journals."

His eyes grew wide. "You have?" He leaned forward again, eyeing her intently. "You've read about Dudleytown?"

"Yes."

"Then you know about the curse of the Dudleys."

"The curse of the Dudleys," she said in a spooky voice, waving her fingers spider-like at him. He didn't laugh, and she felt embarrassed.

"My family used to live up here in Dudleytown," he said. "Several generations ago. You can still see the Bishop house marked on the Dudleytown map at the historical society." She got up to retrieve the pitcher of iced tea. "I don't know exactly when—early 1800s maybe—they moved down the mountain to Cornwall and never came back up here."

She refilled their glasses. "The curse?"

He looked at her for a long while. Did he think that she was mocking him again? She wasn't, although the idea of a curse seemed a bit too Stephen Kingish for her.

Finally, he spoke. "Yes. I guess it was the curse, or at least that's what they called it back then. Jeremiah Bishop was the one who made the move, saying that there were demons up here, preying on the villagers."

"Demons? According to Mister O'Neil's journals, that's what other people have said as well."

"Right."

He looked out the window again and this time, her eyes followed. There was nothing to see out there, other than the eternal woods, but Nathan's intense concentration upon the trees chilled her.

"Look, Nathan, is there a reason why you're trying to scare me?"

Suddenly, he reached over and took her hand, an impulsive move that surprised her, but also felt good at the same time. He looked into her eyes and she saw sadness there. "I'm not trying to scare you, Sandy, really I'm not." He squeezed her hand lightly and she felt the warmth of his hand radiate through her. "I'm sorry. It's just that Ted was a good friend and I worry about people staying up here."

"I don't understand."

He sighed but continued to hold her hand. "I know you don't. Leslie doesn't either, although she may know more than she realizes."

"About what? I don't understand?"

He released her hand and stood. Outside, the shadowed woods watched him, waiting. He could see that she was exasperated with him. He wasn't making sense. Of course not. Were the situation reversed, he would be wondering about her sanity just as much as she was probably wondering about his at this very moment. He had tried to protect Ted and had failed, but he wouldn't let that happen again. Not to Leslie. Not to Sandy. Not to anyone.

He turned to her. "I don't know if there is a curse of the Dudleys or not, but I do know that many people have come to bad ends up here."

"I told you I've read the journals."

"Yes, and yet you remain, which tells me that you are a rational woman, one not easily spooked by legends and tall tales." He leaned over her, his hands resting on the table, his face mere inches from her own. For a moment, she thought he was going to kiss her and, guiltily, she found herself hoping for that. But he did not kiss her. "I consider myself to be a sane and logical man, Sandy, but some things I cannot explain. There is a presence up here. I know it."

"A presence?" she said, quietly, as though afraid to call whatever it was forward by speaking louder.

"A ghost," he said.

NINE

She studied his face. He wasn't growing horns or foaming at the mouth. She looked for a smile, but there was none. He wasn't joking. "A ghost?"

He sat back down and moved the glass on the table aside. "How much of Ted's journal did you read?"

"Not much, I guess. I wanted to read more but didn't know if I should or not. I thought it was personal. An invasion of privacy."

"I understand. Then you may not have read about the sachem."

"The sachem? No, I don't remember that. What's a sachem?"

"Something like a chief. Before the first English settlers came to this area, it was used as hunting grounds by Mohawk Indians, although some say they were Mohegan. In any case, the Indians and the settlers were able to get along for a while, but as it happened all throughout New England, the growth of the English towns and farms required more and more land. Often, the settlers bought the land from the Indians without any problems, but sometimes there was trouble."

"Trouble? And that happened here?" Sandy guessed.

"Yes. The settlers purchased some of the land from the Indians, but the sachem that negotiated with them did not want to give up the land that later was settled as Dudleytown. The sachem's name was Namquid. He claimed the land was sacred ground and could never be sold."

"But it was sold."

"Not quite," he said, shaking his head. "The settlers took control of the property alright, but only after Namquid's decapitated body was found in Bonney Brook."

She felt a sudden dull ache in her stomach, as though an invisible fist had punched her. Decapitated. The gory image that came to her mind lodged there and she could not shake it loose.

"No one was ever accused of the crime," Nathan said, "but it was enough for the Indians to move away. They believed the land had been cursed by Namquid, who was not only a sachem but a shaman as well. The Indians thought if the settlers still wanted the land after that, then good riddance to them. They thought it was cursed."

The pain had subsided, although she still felt slightly nauseous. Her skin felt clammy.

"Are you okay?" he asked. She nodded. "No, you're pale," he insisted. "Maybe you should lie down."

The idea sounded good to her. She stood and found that her legs were wobbly. Before she knew it, Nathan was there and had one arm around her waist, steadying her. "Here, I'll help you to the couch."

She let him assist her into the living room. "I'm sorry," she said, as she lay on the couch, settling a pillow beneath her head. "I don't know what happened to me."

He sat on the couch across from her. "That's okay. Does that feel better?"

"I guess so. But go on, tell me the rest of the story. Where does the ghost come in?"

He eyed her warily. "Are you sure?"

"Yes."

"Alright. Despite what you would think, the ghost is not Namquid, at least I don't think it is. Namquid said this land was sacred because it was inhabited by the Spirit Eater, an evil ghost that preyed upon men's spirits, *souls* we would say. The legend says that the murder of Namquid was a trigger of sorts that set the Spirit Eater loose. Some say that at the moment he was murdered, Namquid cursed his killers, thereby unleashing the Spirit Eater upon them."

"That's a colorful legend."

"It's no legend."

"You said that you knew there was a presence up here. You said it was a ghost. How can you be sure?"

He turned to look out the windows at the rear of the room. The tops of the trees were streaked with sunlight, but further down below, shadows smothered the light, overtaking the woods. A small white owl suddenly came into view, flying over the clearing and disappearing into the trees. He turned back to her.

"I've seen it," he said quietly, and she thought she heard a touch of embarrassment in his voice. He looked at her, waiting for her reaction.

She believed him. She had long ago given up on established religions and their stodgy adherence to dogma that required unflinching belief from the faithful, even if such dogma could never be proven. While resigning from religion, though, she had not given much thought to spiritual matters, certainly not to ghosts, spirits, and demons. Yet, there was conviction in Nathan's voice and in his demeanor. He was certain of what he had seen.

Gingerly, she sat up on the couch. "Tell me about it," she said.

"I used to have a chocolate lab, a beautiful dog named Grendel. She was something," he said wistfully. "One day I had come up here to visit with Ted. I brought Grendel along and let her run around while I spoke with Ted. She was a good dog. She never went far and would come when I whistled for her. But that day, when I was ready to leave, I couldn't find her, and she didn't come to my whistle, so I got in the truck and drove slowly down the road, calling her name and whistling for her through the window.

"I thought I saw movement in the bushes, so I pulled over and got out of the truck. Suddenly, I heard a high-pitched yelp and I knew at once that it was Grendel. I ran a few yards into the woods where I had heard the sound and there she was, lying dead on the ground."

She saw him blink away tears. She was moved by the obvious love he had for his dog and found her own eyes damp.

"I just stood there, looking at her." He looked up at her. "I was stunned. What had happened to her? Then I saw it. I hadn't noticed the cellar hole nearby, but now, a large misty shape was rising from it, hovering in the air above the hole. It was incredible, Sandy! As I watched, it took on the rough form of a man, but a tall man, maybe over six feet tall. It lacked features, though, and was ill-defined. It was more the idea of a man than an actual man.

"I was scared. That's putting it mildly, I guess. Terrified." He laughed nervously. "I couldn't move. The thing seemed to become more transparent and I noticed it was filled with tiny golden lights. They were sparkling. It didn't make any sound, and, despite the lack of facial features, I had the distinct impression that it was looking at me. More, I thought it was coming for me. I snapped out of my trance and ran for the truck. I jumped in and gunned it down the road, leaving poor Grendel behind."

She didn't know what to say. The story was incredible, fantastic, yet it was obvious he believed it. Who was she to say that his experience was all in his head?

"But the worst part," he said, interrupting her thoughts, "was that I never again saw Ted O'Neil alive. Three days later, they found his body."

He should not venture out into the woods, not now, not when the returning owls were calling to each other nervously, incessantly, not when they were so skittish, darting here and there through the trees. Something was wrong, and he had been a part of these woods long enough to know that he should trust their instincts.

That was what he thought even now, where he hid in the bushes, his skin prickling as though alive in every way to whatever was loose in the woods, whatever may be at this very moment standing behind him. Thinking about it, he cautiously turned his head to look behind him. Nothing. The eternal shadows of the dark woods, the agitated owls here and there, but nothing more.

Yet, here he was once again, watching the house, watching as the Mountain Man—the man who seemed to know these woods almost as well as he—drove away in his truck.

The Yellow Lady was alone.

His hand trembled where he held the bush. Fear? Excitement? A wild storm raged through his head, thoughts and images tumbling one over the other, swirling in a crazy whirlwind that made no sense and there, now and again, as if suddenly illuminated by jagged lightning, the woman from so long ago—when, he could not remember—screaming, screaming, screaming . . .

He clapped his hands over his ears, his eyes tightly shut, trying to block out the awful sound. He heard a low sorrowful keening, an animal in pain, and realized the sound rose from his own throat.

Gradually, the sounds died away, vanishing with the image of the unknown woman. Yet, he felt she was not unknown, not really, but was perhaps someone from his past, although "past" had little meaning for him. Whoever she was, the woman reminded him of the Yellow Lady, who, he remembered, was now alone in the house.

He hesitated for a moment, afraid to come out from the cover of the bushes, afraid to make himself a target. But, the Yellow Lady—she *must* be magic, he thought—drew him out, just as she drew him to the house so often, and he was powerless to resist. She wanted him to come to her.

He slipped through the bushes, drawing closer to the house. Although it was mid-afternoon, the interior of the house was dark. A small pool of sunlight puddled on the deck, but the rest of the house was lost in shade. He was just one more shadow as he moved closer. The Yellow Lady was nowhere to be seen. It was easy to enter the house. One moment he was outside, the next he was standing in the living room.

Sandy lay on her belly on the bed in the loft, propped up on her elbows, reading, or trying to read, more of Ted O'Neil's Dudleytown journal. She could not concentrate, though, as she thought of Nathan. His story was hard to believe, but he sounded convincing. That was the scary part, to think that a man who seemed so rational and intelligent could believe in ghosts. And what if—crazy as it seemed—his story was true? What if there was a ghost in Dudleytown?

A chill came over her. If she truly believed that, she would be off the mountain in a flash, wouldn't she? Nathan believed it and continued to come up here; that didn't make any sense, unless he thought he was some kind of guardian protecting Leslie, even if she only came up here sporadically.

These thoughts distracted her from the journal, but there was more. She pictured Nathan in her mind; his strong, tanned arms and legs, his hazel eyes, the way he smiled at her. She remembered the comforting feel of his arm around her waist when he had helped her to the couch. She felt stirrings inside her, the kind of emotions she should not feel if she was still with Kevin . . . was she still with Kevin? Too much to think about right now, she thought, as she returned to the journal.

He looked around the living room and saw it was as it had always been. There were a few books on the table between the couches and two empty glasses. He walked to Leslie's room and looked in. There was no one there. He passed the kitchen and stood at the foot of the stairs to the loft, his head cocked to one side, listening.

In his head, the Yellow Lady was calling him.

She looked up from the journal. What was that? She turned on her side and looked toward the stairs. Had she heard something? She waited a few seconds, listening, but there was nothing to be heard. Damned ghost stories, she thought, they're making me jumpy.

The Yellow Lady waited for him in the loft. She called to him. He would go to her. He placed one foot upon a step, then the other. He felt intense excitement now, so close to the Yellow Lady. Her magic enveloped him like a shroud. Slowly, he began to ascend the stairs.

There it was again. She closed the journal and sat up on the bed, her heart pounding. A footstep on the stairs, that's what she heard, she was certain. She sat there, paralyzed. She wanted to run, but where? The only way out was down the stairs. She could jump over the low wall of the loft. Yes, she could do that and maybe break her leg in the fall. She kept her eyes on the head of the stairs and grabbed her cell phone. Nathan, Nathan, had she remembered to put his number in her phone?

She heard more footsteps on the stairs.

He reached the top of the stairs and there she was, the Yellow Lady, so close he could see the beads of sweat upon her pretty face. For a long moment, he stood there, gazing at her. He looked into her blue eyes and she looked right back at him. She did not speak, she did not move, but only sat there looking at him. Or did she? He had the odd sensation that she was looking at him, but not seeing him. It was almost as though her focus was concentrated on some point beyond him, as though she was looking right through him. He was confused. Why didn't she speak? Why didn't she acknowledge his presence?

She heard the footsteps stop at the head of the stairs, but there was no one there. She sat with the cell phone in her hand, ready to dial it, but there was no one there. Slowly, she stood and walked toward the stairs. Her heart was running rabbit. She couldn't believe that she had not screamed, but screamed at what? She felt a chill, no, a meat-locker cold suddenly surrounding her. She saw her breath condense in the air. Incredible! It was summer!

She was afraid, yes, of course, but she felt more than fear. She was transfixed, fascinated. She raised one hand and moved it through the frigid air as though pushing against an invisible wall. The air felt thick as molasses.

The Yellow Lady stood before him, mere inches away, but she did not see him. He knew that now. Why couldn't she see him? Could she not use her magic? She raised one hand and slowly pushed it forward through the space between them, and then right through him, sending an electric jolt stuttering through his body. Her power was tremendous. He felt as though it would obliterate him, shatter him to particles like a vase struck by lightning. She withdrew her hand and the sweet pain within him subsided.

But there was another, greater pain. She did not see him. She had called him to her and yet, he was invisible to her, nonexistent. That should not be. She was the Yellow Lady, the magic lady. He felt overtaken by sadness. He lifted a hand and gently touched her yellow hair. Then, he was gone.

She felt a breeze, no more than a butterfly's touch upon her hair. She stepped back and in the air before her, saw a disturbance like heat waves radiating from a paved road, and a sliver of light, and then, everything returned to normal. The temperature rose immediately and the animal instincts that had been controlling her body yielded once again to her rational mind. She felt no fear, only wondrous amazement.

TEN

What had just happened? She looked around the loft, peered down into the living room. It was obvious she was alone in the house. Something had been there with her, though, if only for a moment. A ghost? Some might jump to that conclusion after hearing Nathan's story, but that's what the power of suggestion was all about, putting ideas into your head you would not have come to on your own. Advertisers—her clients—knew all about that magical power.

There she was, alone in the woods, reading a journal about spooky happenings in Dudleytown after hearing a ghost story from Nathan. Is it any wonder she would jump at the slightest sound, even if that sound was merely the house settling its old bones? Or that she would feel cold in a house on a mountain shaded by trees, or that shadow and light could surprise her with optical tricks? Ghosts? That explanation seemed unlikely, far-fetched. Maybe it wasn't that something had been there with her, as much as she simply was aware of sudden changes in the environment around her—the sounds of the house, cold, shadowed light—that taken together made it seem like something was there. The power of the mind again, far more plausible.

She still held the cell phone in her hand. Maybe she should call Nathan, anyway, and tell him what she had experienced. He would probably be interested, and her story might help him think differently about his own story, which, the more she thought about it, the crazier it seemed. Yes, maybe they'd even share a laugh over it all.

As she started to punch in his number, she heard the little voice inside her head teasing her: *That's why you want to call him? Really? It has nothing to do with the fact that you might have the hots for him? Do you think I'm stupid, girl?*

"Shut up," she said, aloud. She smiled when he answered. She didn't give him all the details, just enough to arouse his interest.

"Maybe you should get out of there for a while," he said. He was worried about her and she liked that. "I'm over at Buxton's. Do you want to meet me here and we can talk about it?"

Twenty minutes later, she parked her BMW beside his truck at Buxton's store. Before she had time to get out of her car, he came out of the store.

"Saw you pull up," he said, through the open window of her car. "Are you alright?"

The hazel eyes reflected his concern for her. His gaze penetrated her, flooding her with warmth. "Yes, I'm fine. Confused, maybe, but fine."

He suggested they take a little walk up the street to the Red Bridge Café. "It'll be quiet there. We can talk in peace."

It wasn't a long walk but, other than her previous visit to Buxton's, it was the only time Sandy had been on foot in the town of West Cornwall. As towns go, it was tiny but charming; the red nineteenth-century covered bridge spanning the foaming Housatonic River, the graceful white steeple of an old church, the lovely little stone library. The town was situated on a plain and the perspective of Coltsfoot Mountain rising from it in the distance struck her in an odd way. Somewhere up there, lost in that deep green sea, was Leslie's house, completely invisible to anyone living below. It was as though the house and town were in different worlds, different dimensions. That would make her an alien in the town, she thought with a laugh, but she had to admit that after a few days on the mountain, the little town below seemed like Oz.

Nathan held the door open for her as they entered the café. They found a corner table near a window where the sunlight—such as she rarely saw on the mountain—streamed in as though shot from a cannon. An older woman came to take their order, addressing Nathan by name. No surprise, she thought. In a town as small as Cornwall Bridge, everyone knew everyone else.

"So, tell me," he said. "What happened?"

She told him everything, trying to recall the event in all its details, stopping only once when the waitress brought their coffees and a blueberry muffin for Nathan—sweet tooth, he admitted, with a grin. He listened intently without interrupting her, his brow creased in concentration. When she finally finished her story, she sat there, drained, waiting for his response.

Chewing thoughtfully on his muffin, he didn't say anything right away. He washed down the muffin with a swallow of coffee. At last, he said, "But you didn't see anything? You didn't see the figure that I told you about?"

"No," she replied, "nothing. Only that faint shimmer of light that I mentioned, but that wasn't anything like what you described."

He nodded. "You're right. It's not."

A young couple entered the café. The man half-waved at Nathan and he raised his hand in return. They sat across the room, but Nathan lowered his voice when he spoke to Sandy. "I sort of wish you had seen the thing I had witnessed."

"Why?"

"Because then I'd know that we were talking about the same thing. Then I'd know that there was only one ghost."

She looked at him, trying to get her mind around what he was telling her. Impossible, he couldn't mean that. "You're telling me there is more than one ghost up there?" He didn't answer but his expression told her, yes, that was exactly what he was saying. "And here I am telling you that I don't even believe what I saw was a ghost, let alone a member of a family of ghosts."

"I know," he said, softly. "It's hard to believe."

"You think?" she said, unable to control her annoyance. "Nathan, this is not only difficult to believe, it borders on the insane. I thought maybe after I told you my experience and what I thought had caused it, that you might reconsider your own ghost story."

He sat back and shook his head. "No, I know what I saw."

"But you weren't there to see what I saw . . . or didn't see."

"That's true," he said, with a sigh. "Look, Sandy, I'm not crazy. I'm not insane. You're right, I wasn't there. Maybe what happened to you had nothing to do with ghosts. I'm willing to give you that. But, what if you're wrong and I'm right? What then?"

He had suggested, rather strongly she thought, that she remain in town, rather than return to the O'Neil house. There was a nice little bed-and-breakfast place where she would be comfortable, and she knew by "comfortable" he meant "safe." She could see it in his eyes. She was flattered by his interest in her well-being, although she warned herself not to read too much into it. The idea was tempting, but she also thought if she gave in to it, she would be giving credence to Nathan's ghosts. Going back to the house would show him she was not afraid; there simply was not anything to fear except her imagination. He looked so worried when she got back into her car that she almost changed her mind, but she was determined to prove her point.

Now, driving back up Dark Entry Road through the dark tunnel of trees, she fought to hold back her second thoughts about returning. No, it's only your imagination. Let it go. She had her work to do and she had to sort out her feelings about Kevin. She had plenty to keep her mind occupied. And that would start right now, she thought, as she approached the house and saw Kevin's Camaro parked on the road. Shit.

The door of the Camaro opened as she pulled into the drive beside the house and Kevin stepped out. Mirrored sunglasses, black jeans, black shirt, black shoes, he looked like a character from a Quentin Tarantino movie. Had he always dressed like that? Funny that she couldn't remember.

He smiled and took off the sunglasses, sliding them into his shirt pocket. Walking toward her, he opened his arms. "Baby," he said, "how have you been?"

She allowed him to put his arms around her, but when he tried to kiss her, she pulled back. "No," she said, softly.

"No?" He released her. "You're still angry."

"How did you find me?"

Kevin grinned. "You're not that hard to figure out, Sandy."

Was he mocking her? He was still smiling, but there was something behind that smile that made her uncomfortable. "What are you doing here?"

"I thought that would be obvious. I've come to take you home. You remember home, don't you? New York City? Tall buildings, lots of people, sirens, no trees?"

"Don't be a smartass."

His smile vanished. "You're right. I'm sorry. But I miss you, Baby. I want you to come home."

She sighed. "Kevin, I've been thinking about us, thinking about the time . . ."

"Stop." He raised his hand like a traffic cop, "I know what you're going to say. Look, I don't know what came over me at that time. I've told you that before. Hitting women is not my thing, you know better than that. Maybe I was a little cranked up, you know? A little stressed out."

"Maybe you were," she said, leaning back against her car.

He ran one hand through his hair. "Come on, I'm not like that. I've apologized for that a million times and I'm apologizing again, right now. I'm sorry, Baby. I really am."

He seemed sincere. Standing there shifting from one foot to the other, he looked like a nervous schoolboy waiting outside the principal's office. She wanted to laugh, and she would have, had she been able to erase the memory of his hitting her from her mind. But she couldn't do that. It reminded her too much of the life her mother lived with her father. There was no way she would settle for a life like that. But that was her baggage, wasn't it? Was it fair to pin it on Kevin? What if his outburst was truly a once-in-a-lifetime event? Did she want to sacrifice the two years they already shared and a future with him because of one little mistake? Everyone made mistakes. She was so confused and his standing there before her didn't clear up anything.

"Kevin, I . . ."

"All I want is for us to be together," he pressed, sensing her confusion, Somehow, his arms were around her once again. "I miss you. Everyone misses you. They're all asking me where you've gone, when you'll be back. I never know what to tell them."

"How about telling them it's none of their business?" Why did he care what other people thought, anyway? This was between the two of them, no one else mattered. "They just care about you, Baby, that's all." She didn't respond. He took her silence as a good sign; she was thinking things over. He continued to hold her and, while she didn't exactly melt in his arms, she didn't pull away either. "So, what do you say? Are you ready to come back?"

There was something flippant in his tone that seemed to make light of the whole situation. Did he think it was just *that time of the month*, the excuse so many guys used to avoid trying to understand their women? Maybe he thought she was just being *emotional*. After all, women were all that way, weren't they, essentially deranged and in need of men to keep them in line? She hadn't thought Kevin was that kind of man, or at least, not an extreme chauvinist, but now she wondered if perhaps she had been wrong about him all this time.

"We don't have to head back right away. If you like, we can stay here for another day or two. I guess it wouldn't kill me." He smiled. "I've got my bag in the car."

"No," she said, pushing his arms away and standing up straight. "I'm not ready for this, Kevin. I don't know that I'll ever be."

"Give it a chance, Baby. Give this a chance," and he suddenly moved close to her and kissed her before she could turn away.

His lips on hers were not unpleasant and they stirred up old memories, pleasurable memories, but then there was tongue and another hardness pressing against her. She pushed him off her. "No!"

He stood there looking at her and in his eyes, she saw both desire and anger. She didn't want to hurt him, not really, and she certainly didn't want to make him angry. "I'm sorry, Kevin," she said. "Not yet."

That word "yet" formed in his mind like a life preserver and he clung to it. He recognized her indecision and, despite his lust for her, was wise enough to back off. Patience was called for now. "You don't want me to stay with you?" he said, softly, trying on the best hang-dog expression he could muster.

She shook her head. "No, not now."

"Alright, then. Here's what I'm going to do. I'm going to go back down to the village and find a place to stay. I want you to think about us, think about what you want to do. I'll give you a day, but after that, I'm going back to New York, with or without you. Hopefully, with," he added.

"Make it two days?"

"Two? Why two?"

"I don't know." She realized how stupid that sounded. Was she merely postponing the inevitable?

He looked at her for a few moments, considering. "Fine, whatever. Two days. No more."

She nodded her head and he turned and walked away, slamming the door of the Camaro after him. She watched the car spray gravel as it sped away.

ELEVEN

He suddenly awoke with a start, jolted to consciousness by a dream so vivid, he felt as though he was living it. The dream confused and frightened him, yet at the same time, it called to him in a way no dream had ever done. There was a woman, a beautiful woman with golden hair who held him and smiled at him and called him her "sweet-boy." There was a house and woods all around and he heard someone chopping wood, the sound of the ax thunking into the wood growing louder with each stroke. He knew this woman was his mother, but then she was clutching him close, her face contorted, her eyes wild as she whispered frantically into his ear something about protecting himself, about running for his life, hiding, and it was then that he thought of her as a witch. He saw an ax arcing through the air, seemingly of its own volition, but then, everything was lost in a green luminosity speckled with tiny sparks of light.

He leaned against the white stone at the back of the shack, peering into the darkness as though there was something to see, his heart racing. The stone was familiar, comforting. He ran his fingers over the cold surface, tracing what remained of the letters incised upon it and suddenly, a name came into his head: *Lucinda.*

Mother? The witch, the woman with golden hair, Lucinda, all came together as mother, his mother. It was as though a gust of wind had blown away the leaves upon an autumn pond and now he could see clearly to the bottom. *Mother!* For the first time in his memory, there was another person, another name, to which he felt a connection. It had only been him, alone on the mountain, for as long as he could remember. He had always been there, like the rocks an eternal part of the mountain. But now, as if by magic, he was shown something else, a glimpse into a past he did not know he had. He was connected, no longer adrift. But, what more was there?

He closed his eyes tightly as he pressed closer to the stone, trying to recall more details from his dream and he saw, for only a moment, a man in the shining green light, his face apoplectic with rage and madness, and he saw an ax in the man's hands. The image was gone in an instant, but it filled him with dread because in that brief interval another name came to him and it was *Father*.

No! No! No! He slapped his hand against the stone like a child and the images disappeared, replaced only by the silent darkness in the shack. His head hurt. It felt as though he had been pounding it against the stone. He massaged his temples, trying to smooth away the pain and, after a while, the pain had left him.

He did not know how long he remained there, resting against the stone, his mind turning in a million different directions at once, but light began seeping into the shack and he heard the occasional mournful *hoo-hoo-hoo-hoooo* of an owl. Now, fully awake, a deeper mystery than his dream weighed upon him.

How was it that the Yellow Lady did not see him? She had called him, hadn't she? Yet, she was unaware of his presence in the house. Not only did she not see him, she put her hand right through him! That was impossible. There was no magic that would allow her to do such a thing, but it happened, he was sure of that. He felt a shock when her hand passed through him, as though he had been struck by lightning. Even though he stood only inches from her, despite the fact that he had touched her hair, it was as though he simply did not exist for her. They may as well have been in different worlds. For the Yellow Lady, he was no more than . . . a ghost.

No, that couldn't be. He looked at his hands, his feet. He ran his hands over his face feeling the nose, the lips, the eyes. He was solid, he was whole, he was real, wasn't he?

But she didn't see him! Could it be that the Yellow Lady was no more than a dream? No, she was real, as was the Lady, the Mountain Man, and the others he had seen on the mountain. They were real, all of them.

And Mother and Father? What of them? They were dream people, yes, but he was connected to them. Their stories intertwined in some way with his own, but they were no longer in the world. What did that say about him?

He sat up and looked at the stone, something he had done countless times before. This time, it was as though the stone could talk to him. The carved letters seemed to glow as he picked them out again.

Q . . .nt. . . Rand. . . 1868.

Randolph. He didn't know how he knew that name, but it came to him as though he had always known it, and it occurred to him the name might be his own. In his mind, he saw again Lucinda, the beautiful woman with golden hair and the angry man. He knew he was their son. Why that recognition would come to him now, after so long—was it so long?—he did not know, but he sensed there was a reason for his sudden understanding, a reason that would be revealed to him, just as these names had been revealed.

But could it be possible that he really was their son? If that was true, then he would be very old, wouldn't he? Was that possible? Coldness settled over him like a shroud and he began to understand. He was saddened to think that what he called his life was no more than a shadow, his real-life forgotten long ago. He laughed bitterly and wondered if anyone could hear the laughter of a ghost.

Two days? Fuck that! There was something going on with her—something she wasn't telling him. He was sure of that. Another guy, maybe? If that was the case, he wasn't about to let the bitch make a fool of him. And he sure as hell wasn't going to sit on his ass in this godforsaken shithole of a town just waiting for her highness to make up her mind. He'd keep an eye on her, get the facts for himself.

So, only a few hours after he had left her and checked into the Mountain View B&B Kevin was in the Camaro again, driving back up Dark Entry Road. He drove slowly, trying to keep the noise of the car to a minimum. It was late afternoon by that time and the shadowed forest already made it seem more like night. He remembered seeing a narrow road, not much more than an overgrown path, really, intersecting Dark Entry Road before he came to the house. This time, he turned down the path and carefully drove about a hundred yards or so, wincing every time a tree branch brushed the car. *God-damn it!* They better *not* have scratched the paint, he thought. Satisfied that the car was hidden from the view of anyone on Dark Entry Road, he got out and locked it.

Skirting the edge of the road, Kevin walked back up to Dark Entry Road and followed it toward the house. There wasn't anyone else on the road, but he kept close to the woods just in case. He didn't think he had parked all that far from the house, but the walk seemed to take forever. The rugged terrain, studded with rocks and potholes didn't help. Finally, he saw the house in the distance, lights already turned on against the advancing gloom.

He stayed wide of the house and pushed deeper into the woods. He swore as brambles snagged on his jeans and a low-hanging branch scratched his arm. The things he did for that bitch, he thought; she really didn't appreciate him. He circled around the house until he found a vantage point hidden among some boulders that allowed him a good view of the front of the house. The trees around him formed a cocoon of shadow over his observation post, rendering him nearly invisible.

He sat down on a small rock behind the boulders He couldn't remember a time when he was ever so uncomfortable, but he took a perverse pride in his discomfort. It just proved how much he was willing to do for her, for her love. Would Sandy do the same for him? He doubted it.

He sat there, listening to the damned owls hooting in the trees. They were like ghosts, for the most part unseen, until one of them would suddenly glide into view for a few seconds, a floating white form disappearing quickly into the woods. Here, in the woods, it was unseasonably cool, and he was glad he had thought to bring a flask with him. He pulled it out of his pocket and took a swig. The whiskey felt good going down, warming his insides. He took a few more swallows, swatting at gnats and mosquitoes in between. *Shit! They'll eat me alive!* And, with his luck, he was probably surrounded by poison ivy.

The whiskey relaxed him, and the insects became less bothersome. He sat watching the house, imagining what she might be doing. As it grew darker, the lights inside the house seemed brighter, but they revealed nothing of interest. The BMW was parked out front, so she was home, but still, he had not seen her. *Where the fuck was she?*

He didn't know how long he watched, but it seemed hours. It was dark now, the only light coming from the windows of the house, shining like beacons to home-sick sailors. Finally, he saw a shadow pass by a window, or at least he thought he saw a shadow, admitting that his whiskey-induced haze might be responsible for it. But, no, there it was again.

What was she doing?

He looked at his watch. Ten-thirty. Her usual routine would be a hot bath at about that time, then to bed where she might read for a while before falling asleep. Is that what she was doing now? He thought of her getting ready for her bath. He could see her stepping out of her jeans, unbuttoning her blouse, standing there for a moment in bra and panties, and then stripping them off. *Jesus!* He could see her examining herself in the mirror, smiling at the upthrust swell of her breasts, the rounded hills of her ass. Damn, he missed all that. She was one fine piece for sure, no matter how much of a pain she could be. It had been several days now, and he was entitled, wasn't he? *Who the hell did she think she was?*

He rose unsteadily from his hiding place and stood there gazing at the house, knowing that in the darkness of the night he was invisible. All she needed was a little shot of Kevin Perillo and everything would be fine. Maybe she had forgotten what he could do for her, how he could make her feel. Yeah, she'd remember alright, and everything would be as it used to be. He stumbled over a root as he walked toward the house. The house loomed before him, seeming to grow larger, and the bright windows were like magnets, drawing him to them. He stopped short of the front step and made his way to a window, trying to keep his balance.

He cautiously peeked into the window which gave him a view down the front entry into the parlor beyond. The lights were all on in that room, but there was no Sandy. He leaned against the wall, keeping one eye focused on the room. He could smell the alcohol on his breath as he pressed his face against the glass. Suddenly, there she was. She walked into the room, a book in one hand, and sat on a couch. She was barefoot; her long hair pulled back loosely and held with a red band. Unlike the Sandy in his imagination, she was not naked but wore khaki shorts and a green tank top. But, imagination aside, he knew all too well the body that was under those clothes, and that body belonged to him. It was time to reclaim his possession.

With effort, he pushed away from the window and stumbled to the front door. Quietly, he tried the knob, only to find it locked as he thought it would be. No problem. He took out his wallet and removed a credit card. If this door had the kind of cheap lock that most of them did, the card would open it easily, even in the hands of an intruder that had been drinking. After a few tries, he was able to carefully slide the card into the door jamb. He fiddled around with the card until he heard the lock click open. One more shot of liquid courage, though, before he entered the house. He drained the flask. It went down smooth as silk.

He slowly turned the knob and eased the door open a crack. He saw her on the couch, engrossed in her book. Keeping his eyes on her all the time, he slowly pushed the door open just enough for him to slide through, then closed it behind him. He took one tentative step down the entryway. She did not seem him. Another step. Two more before she finally looked up from her reading.

"Kevin!" She jumped up from the couch, dropping the book on the floor.

"Hi, Baby."

"What the hell are you doing here? How did you get in?" Her eyes darted around the room, as though she was looking for someone or something. "Get out! You promised."

He waved the air as though shooing away a fly. "Promise? Yeah, I guess, but Baby, I knew you didn't mean it." He stumbled another step closer.

She could see that he was drunk. "Kevin," she said, trying to reason with him, "you're drunk. Maybe you should just go back and sleep it off."

"Nah, that's no good. I'm fine. He was now in the parlor. "Been thinking about you, Baby, you know that? Been thinking about you and me, been thinking about what it's like when we fuck."

The rude words hit her like a slap. She was in trouble. She could see it in his eyes. She took a step back from him, searching the room again for something that might help her. But help her do what?

"You remember that, don't you, Baby? Yeah, you know." He came closer. She stepped back. "I'm here to remind you." He leered at her, swaying on his feet. "So, why don't you just get naked?"

He reached for her.

"Kevin! No!" She pushed him away. She backed up and hit the coffee table behind her. She lost her balance for a moment and Kevin grabbed her.

"Come on, Baby," he said, smearing his lips against her face.

She struggled with him. Despite his drunkenness, he was surprisingly strong. He held her tightly around the waist with one hand while the other mauled her body, fondling her everywhere, roughly squeezing her breasts, running down between her legs. She scratched at his hands, kicked at his legs and the two of them tottered across the floor like some crippled monster until their feet became entangled and they fell to the floor, Kevin on top.

He grinned down at her. "You like being on the bottom, don't you?" He forced one hand between them and she felt the button on her shorts give way as he pulled. She tried bucking him off, but his weight was too much for her. His right hand came up to her breast. "Love your tits, Baby," he said, squeezing her breast. She cried out in pain.

"Okay, let's do this," he growled. She saw the cruelty in his face that she had always feared was there. Now she knew.

"Kevin, please . . ."

He hit her in the face so hard she thought she would black out. The blow stunned her, and she was unable to resist when he yanked her shorts off. He sat up, straddling her and she could feel his erection pressing against her belly. As if she was watching a film she saw his hands grab hold of her tank top and tear it open as though it was made of tissue paper. She wasn't wearing a bra and the sight of her naked breasts seemed to mesmerize him. In that brief respite, her mind rallied, urging her to fight and to fight as though her life depended upon it. Somehow, she managed to violently twist her body to one side, throwing him off. She was up in a flash, despite the pain in her head. She ran to the kitchen, but he was right behind her. Just as he reached her, she turned and kneed him in the groin. He doubled over in pain, holding his crotch. She pulled a large knife from out of the holder on the counter.

"Kevin," she said, wagging the knife in front of his eyes, her breasts heaving. "Get out!" He looked up at her, his face a mask of fury, but it seemed some of the fight had gone out of him. "I mean it, you bastard! Get out now, or I swear to God, I'll cut your dick off!"

He stood and looked at her for a moment, a sneer crossing his lips before he made his way to the door. She followed him at a safe distance, one hand firmly holding the knife, the other trying to keep closed over her breasts the tatters of her tank top.

"Go on, get out!"

He paused at the door and gave her a look of such hatred she could feel its heat inside her. "You'll regret this, you fucking bitch! And that's a promise I'll keep."

She didn't say a word as he opened the door and staggered out. She slammed it shut behind him, locked it, and watched through the window as he walked down the road and disappeared into the night.

Only when she was sure he was gone, did she collapse on the couch and cry.

Fucking bitch! Fucking bitch! I'll get you. It's not over. Not yet. Kevin seethed with anger as he staggered down the dark road to his car. The moon provided some light, but the deep forest blocked most of it. Twice he tripped and fell and each time he cursed her. *That bitch! What the fuck was wrong with her? Turning a knife on him! Crazy bitch!*

His whiskey buzz was blowing off, but anger raged inside him. His head throbbed in pain, as did his crotch. She would pay.

He came to the road on which he had hidden the Camaro. He started down the road and noticed a strange light in the woods nearby. *Now what?* He was in no mood. He could see the car and the light was growing larger, coming closer. Someone with a flashlight, he thought. But who? He was only a few feet from the car when the light suddenly expanded, filling his vision with a glowing green cloud.

"What the fuck!"

The Camaro was only faintly visible through the cloud which now seemed to be coalescing into some shape. He noticed tiny flecks of golden light sparkling in it.

"Jesus fucking Christ!" he said, as the shape resolved itself into something manlike, something that held what looked like a large club in one hand, a club that swung through the air in a flash, electrifying him into oblivion.

TWELVE

Whatever doubts she may have harbored about her future with Kevin were blown away like ashes in a hurricane. Sobbing and shaking with anger and fear, she curled up on the couch, clutching the torn top around her torso. Never had she experienced such violence. Never. Even in the stormy battles between her mother and father, she had not witnessed such ferocity, such hatred. It was far beyond anything she imagined lived within Kevin. He was out of control. Dangerous.

She looked out the window to the deck beyond. All was darkness. Was he still out there somewhere? She hoped he had sobered up and found his way back to the bed and breakfast—better, back to New York—but he could be stubborn. He might still be out there, waiting for her. She saw the carving knife where she had dropped it on the table. She thought she could have stabbed him if he had not given up, but would she really have been able to do that? Stab someone? She hoped she would never have to find out.

She thought of calling Nathan, but that would be embarrassing. How could she explain her boyfriend troubles to him? Leslie. She needed to call Leslie.

"Call the police!" Leslie immediately said, when she answered the phone and Sandy told her what had happened. "The bastard!"

"Les, I can't."

"The hell you can't! What's the matter with you, Sandy? Are you crazy? The guy tried to kill you."

"Not really. He was drunk, and I don't think he wanted to kill me." There was silence on the phone and in that silence, she heard her own words in her head and realized how weak she sounded, making excuses for him.

"Listen to me," Leslie said, her voice firm. Sandy could see her friend was doing her best to control her anger. "Kevin is dangerous. He had no business breaking into my house and he sure as hell had no business attacking you. Call the police!"

"I can't."

"Call the fucking police."

She sighed. "I don't want to make trouble for . . ."

"Trouble! He's made his own trouble. Sandy, if you don't call the cops, I will."

"Les, please, let me handle this my own way." She was on the verge of crying again. "I want nothing to do with him ever again, but I just want him to go away and leave me alone."

"That's called prison."

"It's over between us, he must know that now. I'm sure by the time he sobers up he'll realize the mistake he made. He'll leave me alone. He wouldn't dare come after me again." At least, I don't think he will, she thought. "I just want to forget that it all happened. I just want to forget about him. I want to get on with my life. If you're truly my friend, you'll let me handle this my way."

"Oh, don't run that 'friend' stuff by me. This has nothing to do with friendship. The man attacked you. Tried to rape you!"

"I'm none the worst for it, a few bruises, that's all. I can live with that."

"You're being an idiot."

"Please, Les." She could feel her friend's frustration boiling over the phone. Leslie meant well, but Sandy knew Kevin better than anyone else; if she made more trouble for him it would not go well with her. He would even the score. She was certain of that now more than ever. "Leslie? Please?"

"I know I'll hate myself in the morning," Leslie finally answered.

Sandy managed a weak smile. "Thanks."

'Where is he now?"

"I don't know."

"You don't know. That's just great. Okay, I'm guessing you've locked all the doors?"

"Yes." She suddenly realized Kevin had entered through the locked front door anyway.

"Okay. Do you know how to use a gun?"

"A gun?"

"Yeah, you know, like in 'bang-bang, you're dead.' A gun, Sandy."

"No."

"My father kept one locked up in the closet in his bedroom. I left it there after he died, for protection when I was at the house."

"I don't know how to use a gun."

"Right, so you've said."

A sudden movement outside the window startled her, a flitting shape in the periphery of her vision. She turned in time to see an owl skimming off into the trees. Damned birds, she thought.

"Sandy, I'm going to drive out there to stay with you."

"That's not really necessary, Les." Still, the thought of having some company right now was comforting.

"Yes, it is."

"I'll be fine."

"You owe me since I'm not going to call the police. So, I'm coming out. Besides, it's my house, remember?"

"Okay." As soon as she said that she felt her spirits lift.

"I'll just throw a few things together and leave."

"It's the middle of the night."

"So? It's only a couple hours to the house. I'll be there before you know it. Just promise me that if he should show up again before I get there you will call the cops, instead of playing the idiot role."

"I don't think he'll be back but, yes, if he does come back, I'll call."

"Right away."

"Yes, right away."

"Okay. Stay put, I'm on my way."

Stay put? Where else would she go? She felt better after talking with Leslie. It was not a long drive from the city and at that hour of the night, there would be little traffic. She did feel guilty about getting her friend involved in her troubles and inconveniencing her like that but what was she to do? She needed someone. She picked up the knife and went upstairs to the loft where she replaced her ruined tank top with a new t-shirt. Still carrying the knife, she went back downstairs and seated herself on a couch that allowed her to see both the deck and front entry simultaneously. The night had already seemed eternally long, and she was both physically and mentally exhausted. But, she needed to stay awake until Leslie arrived.

Dead.

That did not seem possible. It was not that he denied death; he had seen it before on the mountain, but it was his own death that was simply unbelievable. When? How? For perhaps the thousandth time that day he looked at his hands, saw the ropey veins, the dirty fingernails, and the old scar at the base of one thumb where a raccoon had bitten him. The hands were solid, flesh and blood—at least they felt that way to him. He looked down at his bare feet, wiggled his toes. They were real, he was certain.

But he was invisible, intangible to the Yellow Lady. Had she flinched when he stroked her hair? Perhaps, but that was not much of a reaction. He was hardly more than an irritation to her, a whispered breeze and nothing more.

Yet, the owls in the forest saw him. He was real to them, sharing their woods with them and they reacted to him as they would react to any other human being. And then, there were the young people that used to come up to the mountain late at night, armed with all kinds of devices, nervously searching for something in the darkness, often scaring each other silly over the hooting of an owl or a moon shadow suddenly thrown across their path. Those people called out to him, inviting him to show himself, to speak, and, lonely for company, he would try to accommodate them. He thought that some of them had seen him. That proved he was real, didn't it?

But how could he be real to them and not to the Yellow Lady? Real is real, or was he only real when, and if, others saw him? This was all too much to think about. It would have made even an adult's head hurt.

He needed air. He pushed aside the plywood door of his shack and stepped out into the ravine. He breathed in the cool night air and was certain that he felt it deep within him. He looked up and through the tracery of leaves overhead saw the distant pinpoint stars wheeling above him. How many times had he seen those stars?

How could he be dead?

He stepped up out of the ravine and now it appeared to him that his feet hardly touched the earth, that he nearly floated up, and suddenly, he was aware that what he had always accepted as a graceful light tread born from familiarity with his surroundings might be something else entirely. Yes, solid as he felt to himself, there was no denying a lightness of body he had not noticed before.

He felt new worlds, new possibilities immediately opened to him. Had it always been so? It all started with that dream about his mother and father. It was as though the dream had unlocked something inside him, a secret room containing many mysteries not yet revealed. He sensed there was more to come and for the first time ever, he believed there was a purpose to his existence. He didn't know what it was, but that, too, would be revealed.

Dead. How strange.

He aimlessly drifted—that was the only way to describe his movements now—through the trees, one more shadow among many. The darkness filled his being and he felt a part of it. He let whatever force was directing him to have its way as he sailed through the forest like a leaf caught on an autumn breeze. The shack was left far behind him now, but that did not worry him. The mountain had been his home for as long as he could remember. He could always find his way back.

He found himself descending a wooded slope to a small clearing where the moonlight filtered in through the trees. There was a small creek running alongside the clearing, the gurgling water echoing like voices in the night. This was a familiar place, although he had not been there in a long time. Something thudded in his chest as he entered the clearing, a palpable sense of dread thick as fog hanging in the air.

The moonlight revealed several carved stones leaning in the earth. Choked by weeds, pocked by moss and mold, the engravings upon them were worn and, on some stones, illegible. He didn't want to be there, but something had brought him there and demanded that he stay.

Why?

He saw the white form of an owl sitting high up in a tree, motionless, watching him. Then, a second bird glided down from the hill and settled on a branch on the other side of the clearing. He had the absurd notion they were there to speak with him in some way, perhaps to guide him.

But was that any more absurd than his being dead?

Drawn to the stones in the ruined cemetery, he lingered there, reading the inscriptions that were still legible, running his hand over the smooth stones. He thought he recognized some of the names, but he did not know why. He spotted a small stone, only about a foot high, removed from the others. It sat at the foot of a tree where a root had curled around it as though protecting it from unknown dangers.

He moved closer to the little stone and read the inscription, bathed in moonlight: *Will Randolph.* That name! It filled him with anxiety. He knew that name. Below it the inscription read:

> *For Sweet-Boy, sadly taken away,*
> *Be with the angels, this do we pray.*
> *1868*

Pain and sorrow shot through him like lightning. Sweet-Boy, the name his mother had called him in the dream—was it a dream? How long he stood there looking down at the stone that bore his name, a name that was new to him, he did not know. Time stood still as he gazed at the grave-stone—his gravestone—trying to make sense of it all. There were memories pushing at him, clamoring for attention. He could feel them swarming behind the curtain in his mind and then, suddenly, bursting through the curtain, rushing at him awful in their horror.

He saw it, he saw it all, his father Quentin, his face trans-formed into a monstrous beast, his body glowing oddly green, speckled with tiny flickers of light, and the axe in his hand as the father-beast kicked down the bedroom door where he and his mother cowered in fear and his mother screaming for him to *Run! Run, to the woods!* And he ran, barely escaping the monster but seeing in his peripheral vision the ax swing-ing through the air, hearing the last truncated scream of his mother and the thud and roll of something hitting the floor, and the spray of warm blood that splashed his face. And he saw himself run to the woods near the barn, saw the father-beast walking from the house to the barn, covered in blood, entering the barn, saw him climb the rafters, rope in hand and tie one end to a rafter, slip the noose around his neck and step off into space, the heavy body plunging, then jerking to a halt that nearly tore the head from the body, swinging in the air, the head grotesquely skewed to one side, the face black and swollen, eyes popped like hard-boiled eggs. And then he saw the glow, the greenish mist emerging from the body, forming a shape in the air, morphing into the form of an Indian, a transparent, sparkling savage that swiveled its head in his direction and picked him out where he hid in the trees, but he would not look at it because he was afraid and if he did not look at it, then it could not be real and then he ran, and ran, and ran, tears streaming down his face, his breath ragged, until he could run no more and found the ravine.

That was 1868, the year he disappeared into the woods, never to be seen again. He realized the grave before him held no mortal remains. It was empty, merely a memorial to the missing boy, Will Randolph. He had been ten years old. How long would it have taken for the forest to claim him? Sad-ness closed around him like a fist. He had no memories of the end—how it happened, what it felt like—but he mourned just the same for the boy he once was and what he had become.

Dead. So, yes, he was dead and had been for quite some time.

Yet, he lived, in a sense. He was still a boy, but in some ways, he felt like a man, as though he had grown up even in death. But he existed.

Ghost. What else could he be?

Silvery shadows slipped across the damp ground as the moon continued its path through the sky, but he remained there, transfixed to the spot like an ancient oak, thinking. His mind filled with more vague images, flitting in and out like bats. It was as though the old cemetery was calling to him, as if the poor souls buried there were reaching up to him from the rocky soil, clutching at him with bony, spectral fingers, desperately trying to communicate with him. What was it they had to say?

His head filled with light as a jolt of energy suddenly shot through him, rocking him where he stood, and now he saw the others, the cursed people of Dudleytown: the man struck by lightning as he sat rocking on his front porch, the farmer that broke his neck in a fall from a roof beam during a barn-raising, the little girl drowned in Bonney Creek, the senile old man locked in the cellar by his daughter and left to starve, the young man that stabbed to death his own brother in a dispute over a valley girl, the woman that shot her husband in the head for no apparent reason, his own parents Quentin and Lucinda, the man that placed a rifle against his chest and shot himself in the woods, and so many others. He saw them all as a gruesome parade of bloodied, hacked and mutilated bodies, extending back into the past as far as the first Dudleys to reach the mountain, and hovering over the macabre procession like a hellish cloud he saw the Indian, the sachem.

An arrow of fear pierced him because he realized the parade had not yet passed by. The sachem was once again loose on the mountain.

THIRTEEN

Despite her best efforts to stay awake, the emotional trauma of the last few hours had completely drained her. She dozed on the couch, the knife sliding from her grip and clattering to the floor. Someone knocking on the door and the sound of a key turning in the lock startled her awake. She grabbed the knife from off the floor and jumped to her feet. The door pushed open.

"Hello? Sandy?"

Leslie. She felt the tension coiled inside her relax and fade away as she hugged her friend tightly. Even though she had promised herself that she would not cry, the tears came.

"That's alright," Leslie said, stroking her friend's hair, "let it all out."

"I'm glad you came."

"Of course. What would you expect?"

"You're a good friend, Les," Sandy said, releasing her. She sat on the couch and Leslie seated herself across from her.

"Have you seen him since we spoke on the phone?" Sandy shook her head. "That's good, but he's still out there somewhere."

"I know," Sandy said, softly.

"What do you want to do?"

She realized that she was still holding the knife, that, in fact, she had been holding it as she hugged her friend. *Jesus!* She placed it on the table between them. She sat erect, sweeping one hand through her hair.

"I don't want to make trouble for him, as I told you before. I just want to forget about it all, forget about him. I want him out of my life, I'm certain about that, so the best thing is to just ignore him."

"And you still think he'll be okay about being ignored? You think he'll just go away?"

"I hope so."

"Fat chance, I say."

"Les . . ."

"No, don't worry. If that's how you want to play it, I'll go along with you. I think you're crazy, but I'll do what you want. But here," she said, standing up and taking her friend's hand, "come with me. I want to show you something."

Sandy stood, a quizzical expression on her face. "What?'

Leslie led her into her bedroom at the front of the house, the room that had once been her father's. "Open that drawer." She indicated the drawer in the oak nightstand beside the bed.

Sandy opened the drawer. A couple of pens, a notepad, a plastic bookmark, one dead ladybug, and in the back, a white envelope. She removed it from the drawer. It felt heavy.

"Go ahead. Open it." Sandy opened the flap and removed a key. "That key unlocks this box," Leslie said, opening the closet door and removing a metal box from the shelf above the clothes rack. "You open it. I want you to be familiar with it."

Leslie set the box on the bed. Sandy unlocked it and lifted the lid. Snuggled inside a plastic foam liner was a revolver. She stood there looking at it, as though it was a rattlesnake about to strike.

"That was my father's gun. He bought it when he moved out here. It's a .38. Small but effective."

Sandy looked at her friend. "And?"

"And, you should know how to use it. Just in case."

"In case Kevin comes back, you mean." Leslie nodded. "You expect me to shoot him."

"Well, maybe not shoot him, but at least, threaten him, keep him at bay."

"Who's crazy now, Les? Do you really think I could shoot him? Do you think I could shoot anyone? Shit! What's wrong with you?"

"Don't get upset, Sandy. It's only a suggestion."

She pressed her hands to her temples. "I'm not hearing this, I'm not. My best friend suggesting I shoot my ex-boyfriend."

"That's not what I'm saying."

"Sure, it is. That's exactly what you're saying!"

"I'm just trying to help." Leslie felt her own anger rising. "What are you going to do if he comes back for you, huh? Are you going to offer him tea and cookies and invite him to sit down and talk things through? Yeah, that'll work. Maybe you could invite Dr. Phil over as well and the three of you could work it all out."

"He's not that kind of guy."

"That's my point. He's not Mister Sensitive. Not Mister Nice Guy."

"No, I mean he won't come back."

"Really. And that's based on what, exactly?"

She sat on the bed beside the box, feeling the weariness rise in her again. "I don't know, Les, I just don't think he would."

"But you never thought he would hit you either and he did. And now, he's done much worse."

Sandy sighed. "Yes, he has."

Leslie sat beside her and took her hand. "Look, Sandy, all I'm saying is that you need to protect yourself. I've never liked Kevin, you know that. I've never hidden that from you. But now, it seems to me that he's really lost it. He's dangerous."

That was true, no matter what she tried to believe about him. It was painful to accept the truth about him. What did that say about the relationship they had shared for two years? More, what did it say about her ability to judge men? Was she so screwed up that she could not find a better man than Kevin?

"Maybe you're right." She closed the top of the box that held the gun. "But right or wrong, I could never shoot anyone. The most I can do is call the police if he shows up here again. I didn't even want to do that much, but if he is dangerous, I promise I won't take any chances with him. I won't call Dr. Phil."

Leslie laughed, and her laughter sounded like music to Sandy. She began to laugh, too. What else could a person do in such an utterly insane and dangerous situation? Like whistling through a graveyard, their laughter buoyed them and gave them hope that they would somehow emerge safely on the other side.

Even though she had driven to the house from New York the previous evening and had spent much time consoling Sandy throughout the night, Leslie was up early the next morning. That's how it had been when she visited her father here, the two of them rising each morning with the sun to talk a walk in the woods. Old habits are tough to break.

Sandy was still asleep in the loft and, considering all that her friend had been through, Leslie was content to let her sleep. As she filled the coffee pot with water, she looked out the kitchen window at the woods beyond, suffused with pale green light as the sun rose somewhere above the trees. The woods were still, each tree standing like a silent sentinel, their ranks extending back into the forest, finally disappearing in the gloom.

She thought of the many times she and her father had tramped through those woods. How they had enjoyed that time together! But there were changes taking place within her father that she did not know about, alterations in his mental state that ran deep and utterly transformed him. Still, he was good at hiding his feelings from her. She could not have imagined that he would fall victim to a depression so severe that it would cause him to take his own life. Nor could she believe he would be so successful in keeping her from discovering it, considering how close they had been, especially after her mother died. Even when the coroner had confirmed his death as a suicide, she found it difficult to accept that verdict, although she ruled out foul play as well. A freak accident? Possibly, but given the facts, unlikely. Suicide seemed the only plausible explanation, yet knowing her father, it didn't really seem plausible at all. In her mind, her father's death remained unsolved and that lack of resolution ached within her.

Her thoughts were interrupted by the boiling coffee pot. She took a mug out of the cupboard and filled it, the coffee aroma filling the kitchen, making her feel a little better. She thought she heard some movement from the loft; Sandy awakening? Leslie stood in the kitchen, sipping her coffee. She was about to take the mug over to the table when she heard tires crunching up the road toward the house. Setting the mug on the counter she peered out the window. Nathan Bishop's white pickup was making its way up the road.

She went outside to meet the truck.

"Leslie!" Nathan said as he climbed down from the cab. "I didn't know you were here. It's good to see you."

She gave him a hug. "Well, I hadn't planned on coming out. It was sort of a sudden thing."

He eyed her suspiciously. "Sudden? Is everything alright? Is Sandy okay?"

She could hear the anxiety in his voice and his hazel eyes registered concern. Lucky girl, she thought, and she doesn't even know it. "She's fine now."

"Now? What do you mean now?"

She hesitated, unsure of how much of Sandy's personal affairs she should reveal to him, but the decision was taken from her as Sandy appeared in the doorway.

"Hello, Nathan," she said, her voice calm, no trace of yesterday's fear in it.

Both women grew suddenly quiet and Nathan sensed something amiss. He folded his arms across his chest, his biceps taut against his blue t-shirt. "Okay, something's going on."

Leslie looked at Sandy but remained silent.

Nathan knew the mountain better than anyone, Sandy thought. Maybe he should hear the story, just in case Kevin came back. But it was an embarrassing story. What would he think of her once he heard it? She sighed. "You may as well come in, Nathan," she said. "Leslie just made some fresh coffee."

He followed the women into the house, careful to wipe his boots on the porch before entering. Sandy poured coffee for Nathan and herself and the trio took their mugs into the living room.

"What's brought you up here so early this morning?" Sandy said as she sat on the couch.

He placed his mug on the table and sat back on the couch opposite her. "I thought about our last conversation when we met in town."

Leslie shot Sandy an inquisitive look.

He raked his fingers through his hair. "The thing is, I made you angry and that wasn't my intention."

"You didn't make me angry."

He shrugged. "It seemed that way to me. Anyway, I came up here to apologize."

Sandy was aware of Leslie sitting beside her, about to burst with curiosity. "There is no apology needed, Nathan. We simply disagreed about the ghosts."

"Ghosts?" interrupted Leslie, unable to keep herself in check. "What ghosts?"

Sandy turned to her. "I'll explain later," she said. Then, to Nathan, she said, "No matter; ghosts aren't on my mind right now."

He leaned forward. "Go on."

Where do I begin, she wondered. No sense dancing around what had happened. Just get it out. "I was attacked last night, Nathan."

"What?" Instinctively, his hands balled into fists and she saw the muscles in his arms tense as if he was ready for a fight. "What do you mean?"

She described how Kevin had broken into the house and what he had done to her, what he had tried to do to her. She was able to tell her story without becoming emotional, as though she was reading a movie script. All the while that she related her story he sat immobile, intently gazing at her, but clearly ready to spring into action in a second, as though he anticipated another attack to be imminent.

"My god, Sandy!" he said when she had finished her tale. "What did the police say? Did they get him?"

"See?" Leslie said. "What did I tell you?"

"We didn't involve the police," she said.

"We?" said Leslie.

Sandy tried to explain why she had not called the police, but Nathan was slowly shaking his head as she spoke and, hearing her explanation aloud, she realized how lame it sounded. Kevin had beaten her, tried to rape her and, who knows, may have killed her. And she was protecting him?

"Sandy, you've got to go to the police," he said. She was about to speak, but he cut her off. "As I drove up here this morning, I saw a car parked off the road. I was going to ask you about it, but I don't have to now. It was a black Camaro, just like the one you said Kevin was driving. He's still on the mountain."

The women were stunned.

"I was sure he would have left," Sandy finally said. She looked up at him. "Okay, make the call."

He had never seen so many people on the mountain. There were several men in uniforms, wearing gray broad-brimmed hats. One of them was examining tracks in the road while others combed through the weeds and trees. There were three people he recognized standing off to one side, watching the men in uniform; the Lady, the Yellow Lady, and the Mountain Man. What was going on?

He crept closer. He could hear the men talking, but their voices sounded garbled and he could not make out what they were saying. It was obvious they were carefully searching the area for something, but what? Suddenly, his mind was filled with the vision of other men in dirty overalls, beating the bushes and scouring the woods, all the while calling out a name. Just a boy, he lagged behind with the silent women in their long dresses, watching, listening to the men frantically calling, when finally, a strong voice yelled up from the steep hillside leading down to Bonney Creek: *I've found her!* Shortly after, the grim men brought up the body of little Elizabeth Hardy, drowned. He remembered that he had seen a thin green vapor trail behind the men for just a moment before disappearing, but no one else seemed to have seen it and he soon forgot about it.

But now, another search. For what?

Yet another State Police patrol car bumped up Dark Entry Road, joining the other two whose flashing lights streaked the woods in bands of red and blue. Sandy noticed the metal screens in the car's rear windows and watched as the K-9 officer let out his dogs. He led them over to the Camaro parked beneath the trees, where they sniffed and snuffled around the tires. The dogs seemed bewildered, she thought, watching them mill around the car.

"I don't think they're picking anything up," she said.

"Give them time," Nathan said.

"Where do you suppose he would have gone? Why would he leave his car? That's his baby."

The trooper in charge walked over to them. His name tag read *Larsen*. Beneath the broad Smokey the Bear hat, Sandy saw that he was an older man. A sheen of perspiration gleamed upon his brow.

"We've checked the vehicle and the area around it," he said, addressing the group, "but haven't found anything unusual. The car's in good shape, nothing wrong with it, so I can't tell you why it's sitting here. I've already called a wrecker to tow it off the mountain. As for the missing person . . ."

"Kevin," Sandy said.

"Yes, Kevin," Larsen said. "We'll let the dogs do their thing, see if they can find him."

"If they don't find him?" Leslie asked.

"We'll continue to patrol the area, ma'am, in case he turns up, but I'm doubtful he will."

"Why not?" Nathan asked.

"Because he simply left his car here. That doesn't make sense."

"Right, so why do you think he won't be back to get his car?"

Larsen shifted uneasily, but his face, a face that had seen many tragedies over the years, remained inscrutable. "He may be unable to return to the car."

"Unable," Sandy repeated. She understood what he meant.

"Let's see what the dogs turn up first. Then we'll take it from there," the trooper said.

Sweet-Boy watched the dogs snuffling through the weeds. He didn't know what kind of dogs they were, only that they were big and black, with surprisingly gentle eyes. He was close enough to hear them huffing through the foliage. As if he had whistled to them, both dogs jerked up their heads and leveled their eyes at him. They stood completely still, watching him.

"What have you got, boy?" a uniformed man asked, as he came up behind them. "What is it?" The dogs remained fixated upon Sweet-Boy. "What are you staring at?"

Sweet-Boy didn't move, afraid the dogs might come after him. His eyes locked on theirs and then, the dogs began to whine. They began to tremble as if shivering with cold, and one of them tried to bark, but the sound died in his throat like a stifled cough.

"What the hell's the matter with you two?" the man said. "Come on, get moving."

One dog finally managed a frightened bark. As if that was a cue, both dogs dropped their tails between their legs, turned and bolted away, the uniformed man chasing after them, cursing.

Sweet-Boy though it best not to take any more chances with the dogs and found himself back in his shack hidden in the ravine.

It wasn't long before an embarrassed Trooper Larsen returned to the trio standing at the edge of the road. "The dogs didn't turn up anything."

"I heard one bark," Nathan said.

"Yeah, false alarm. Something spooked him, but we didn't find any reason for it. You never know, sometimes they're a bit skittish," Larsen said.

"So, what now?" Sandy asked.

"We've got an APB out on your boyfriend." She winced at that word. *Boyfriend.* Not anymore. "Every trooper in the area will be looking for him."

"That's it?" Leslie said. "That's all you can do?"

Larsen shrugged. "There's not much more we *can* do. We'll run some extra patrols by here, that might help. We'll keep an eye out for him, don't worry."

Easier said than done, Sandy thought.

FOURTEEN

It was as though a dam had burst and now, memories that had been held back for years came roaring forth, washing over him like an enormous wave, threatening to drown him in their swirling depths were it not for the recollected bits and pieces of mental flotsam to which he clung desperately. They were fragments, yes, but they sustained him.

There was the crazy old man Jeremiah Chambers, filthy and gaunt, stumbling around in the darkness of the cellar, mumbling to himself, picking lice off his body and eating them, crushing them between his teeth like nuts, while all the while his sisters sat at table upstairs dining on venison and cabbage and new potatoes, completely oblivious to the cries of the man they had locked in the cellar, slowly starving to death.

There was the woman newly widowed by the Civil War—was her name Faith?—that had listened to the pitiful wails of her baby so long they had driven her to distraction and caused her to take up a pillow to silence the baby's cries.

He saw again an enraged William Shifflet, a Mexican War veteran, as he raised the old Army Colt revolver that had served him so well at Vera Cruz, pointing it at the back of the head of Robert Beech, a longtime friend but now a rival for the love of a lady. He heard the explosion and smelled the burnt powder as though it had just happened, saw Beech fall to the ground and saw Shifflet standing there for a moment horrified, before turning the smoking pistol on himself.

Sweet-Boy saw all these things and more, fragments of the tragic history of Dudleytown, but was mystified by them as well. It was impossible that in his short life he could have witnessed all these tragedies committed over many years and yet, he had memory of them. Is that what it meant to be dead, to be a ghost? Was he, in fact, a silent and unseen witness to these horrible acts of violence? Why?

One more memory came swimming up to him out of the depths and once again, he saw himself running, running through the dark woods, the images of his father's body hanging in the barn, his mother's headless corpse in the bedroom seared into his child's brain as though with a branding iron. He ran headlong through the woods, the thickets tearing at him, scratching him, bloodying him, his breath ragged, his eyes wild, seeing nothing and everything at the same time. He ran until he could run no more. He stopped and fell to the ground, unable to take one more step. He looked back through the gloomy woods, but nothing pursued him. Exhausted, he closed his eyes.

Sweet-Boy saw himself asleep in the woods and remembered the wolves and mountain lions that had roamed the mountain at that time. How long could he have survived? No more images came to him, a blessing he thought since the boy in his vision could not have emerged from the woods alive. He was glad to be spared the vision of his own death.

But he had been here on the mountain all this time, he didn't know exactly how long, kept here, it seemed, for some reason. For the first time that he could remember, he felt sadness, aware of his presence in the woods as being out of time, out of place. He did not belong here. Somewhere, people awaited him, were, perhaps, searching for him. They were his people, his family, and he belonged with them rather than lost here on the mountaintop in the company of owls. Was there a way to find them?

"Don't you think it would be best if you two got a room in town?" Nathan asked as they watched the wrecker pull up the Camaro. A man in greasy coveralls got out of the truck and attached chains to the car, securing it in place on the truck bed. When he was satisfied the car was secure, he slowly maneuvered the truck down the narrow road.

Sandy watched as the green forest swallowed the truck from sight. The State Police troopers had already left and now the three of them stood in the overgrown road. She noticed how quiet the woods had become.

His question echoed what she had already been thinking. It would probably be safer for them in town. Still, the troopers and their dogs had turned up no sign of Kevin. Could he still be on the mountain? Kevin was not the outdoors type and so, she preferred to believe he had simply come to his senses and left the mountain. But the car? What about the car? That didn't make sense. Maybe he was still planning on coming back for it.

There was more, though. If she left the house, driven out of it by Kevin, then she would be admitting defeat. She would be allowing him to control her. If she hoped to make it clear to him that their relationship was finished, then she needed to be in complete control of herself. She needed to be free. No man should ever be able to control her. She would decide how much control she would give to any man and further, she would decide who that man would be. It was clear that man was not Kevin.

She was not a heroine in a novel. Staying at the house would be risky and she was not certain she was brave enough to do it. Leslie was there, yes, but she could not ask her friend to stay with her. She could not put her in danger.

"This is my house, Nathan," Leslie said. "I'm not about to let anyone scare us away."

Sandy took heart when Leslie spoke up so forthrightly. She had always admired her boldness, a quality she thought lacking in herself, but what Leslie was proposing went beyond bold; it was dangerous.

"I know how you feel," he said, "but it would only be for a little while until they catch Kevin. No one's driving you from your house."

She folded her arms across her chest but did not say anything more. Sandy recognized that familiar gesture; she was digging in.

"Les, I know you're saying that on my account," Sandy said.

"The hell I am," Leslie said. "That bastard broke into my house and assaulted you. Besides beating the crap out of you, he violated my space. That makes it personal, Sandy. Just the thought of him creeping around my place makes my blood boil. No, I'm staying."

Once her friend had made up her mind about something there would be no changing it. "Alright, Les, I'll stay with you."

"Ladies . . . ." Nathan said.

"It'll be fine, Nathan, really," Leslie said. "Don't worry about us."

"Of course, I'll worry about you," he said.

"The troopers will be patrolling the area and we'll be careful. We can take care of ourselves." Sandy glanced at her friend. Leslie was referring to her father's gun hidden in the closet. God, I hope it doesn't come to that, she thought.

"I really don't feel good about this, but if that's the way you want it, then so be it," Nathan said.

Sandy saw the lines of worry etched upon his handsome face. She wanted to smooth his furrowed brow and tell him everything would be alright. She wondered what it would be like to run her fingertips over his brow and along the strong line of his jaw, to lightly trace the curve of his lips. She felt heat spread across her face. Get a grip, she told herself, this is not the time.

"Well, it won't just be the troopers on patrol. I'll be checking on you, too."

"Thank you, Nathan," Sandy said.

They walked up the road to the house. Somewhere high up on a ridge an owl hooted. The birds had recently become common in Dudleytown so that Sandy no longer heard their calling to each other, the mournful sounds transforming into a natural white noise. But this time, the solitary call was clear and distinct, resonating inside her as forcefully as if someone had whispered her name in her ear. She looked up along the tree line, trying to locate the white form of the owl in the play of shadow and light where sunlight nuzzled the treetops, but the bird was invisible.

She felt as though her skin had been stripped away, exposing her raw nerves. It seemed she heard every little rustling in the woods around her, saw each and every leaf trembling in the breeze. She could smell sweet honeysuckle, pungent wild onion, and musky vegetation decaying in the damp and loamy forest, a scent so strong she could taste it. Ferns brushed against her bare legs, their feathery leaves like thousands of tiny fingers tickling her. She knew what was happening to her. Fear and anxiety kicked up the adrenaline in her, wired her to be observant and cautious, ready for anything. Oddly, at a time when her life was in danger, she felt more alive than ever before.

"Maybe I should stick around for a while," Nathan said, as they reached his truck parked before the house. Even as he spoke, his eyes scanned the woods.

Sandy laid her hand upon his shoulder. "You're a dear," she said, "but you've done enough already." He looked at her for a moment and there was something that passed between them, an unacknowledged emotion that once again caused her to blush.

He gave her a slight smile. "Okay," he said, opening the door of the cab. He climbed into the truck and pulled the door closed. Through the open window, he said, "Just be careful, both of you. Call me if you need anything and, please, call the police if he shows up again."

Sweet-Boy thought about the men in uniform searching through the woods. He knew what was out there, he had seen it once before and knew it had returned. A story told to him as a boy about an Indian ghost. The Spirit Eater. His mother knew the story and, once more, he heard her telling him all about the curse of the murdered sachem and the ghost he had visited upon the people of Dudleytown. A fairy tale his mother had said, nothing more. Don't be afraid. But he was afraid because his mother had been wrong. He had seen it and he recognized in his mother's last moments, she too had seen the horrible phantom. And now, the Spirit Eater was back.

The forest animals had begun to disappear some time ago, slipping away one by one to another place of refuge, until it became rare for any living creature to cross his path. But the owls were an exception. They not only remained in the woods but seemed to increase in numbers as though filling the void left by the other animals. Their hooting echoed through the trees both day and night. He remembered hearing them on that day so long ago when he ran screaming into the woods.

He thought of Lady and Yellow Lady in the house and the Mountain Man as well. Did they know of the Spirit Eater? And what of the other one? The other man he had seen only briefly before he disappeared. Who was he? Where did he go?

Sweet-Boy was afraid to stay on the mountain, but where else could he go? Something was unfolding before him, he thought, a story in which he was a character, although he did not yet know what he was supposed to do. He felt he was supposed to wait, that the story would continue and carry him along inside it. Perhaps, it would finally reach its conclusion.

"Maybe this wasn't such a good idea," Sandy said, standing by the back windows, watching darkness fall across the clearing. The trees beyond were like a wall, solid and impenetrable. If there was anything out there waiting in the woods, she would never be able to see it. But it could see her, illuminated as she was by the lights behind her. Instinctively, she moved away from the window, a shiver of fear running through her.

"We'll be fine," Leslie said, and even though she had said that repeatedly over the last few hours, Sandy thought she detected a quaver of uncertainty in her friend's voice. She hoped she was wrong; if Leslie lost her nerve Sandy would not be strong enough to go through all this alone.

Maybe Leslie understood that as well, for she suddenly changed the topic. "So, what's all this with you and Nathan?"

"What?"

"You heard me, girlfriend. I saw the looks you two were giving each other. You most definitely mind-fucked him."

"Leslie!"

"Ha! See? I knew it. You're like a window, I can see right through you." Sandy didn't answer. "There's nothing wrong with that, you know. Nathan's a nice guy. Handsome. Unattached. And he's got the hots for you."

"Oh, Leslie, please . . ."

"Well, he does! Quit being such a schoolgirl. You know I'm right."

She didn't know anything of the sort. They hardly knew each other, and her present circumstances were not conducive to a love affair. She was in fear for her life, for God's sake. How could she think of anything else? And yet she did, damn it. She was drawn to Nathan, she admitted that, but so what? Attraction did not equal a relationship.

"What are you going to do about it?"

"Do?" she said, standing near her friend sitting on the couch. "I'm not going to *do* anything."

Leslie sighed dramatically. "Your loss, if you don't, but if he ever looked at me the way he looks at you. . . "

"You're jealous!"

Leslie shrugged. "As if I had a chance. I've known Nathan for a long time and he's never shown that kind of interest in me. I gave up years ago. I think he's yours for the asking. Besides," she said, with a casual flick of her wrist, "he's not my type."

"And what type would that be?"

"I'm thinking an Arab sheik, filthy rich with oil money. Know any?"

Sandy laughed and shook her head. "No, sorry, fresh out of oil sheiks. And you don't want to share him with all the other women in his harem, anyway, do you?"

"I can be bought."

The women laughed, and it felt good. For a few moments, Kevin was far from Sandy's mind.

"You know I'm only teasing you about Nathan," Leslie said, "even though I do suspect something going on there."

"I know, Les. As for Nathan, I really can't be thinking about him right now."

Leslie nodded. "But tell me, what was all that talk about ghosts?

She sat down beside her friend. "It's weird, to say the least. The short story is that Nathan thinks the woods are haunted." Leslie was silent. "No joke, Les? That's not like you."

"No, go on," she said, quietly.

Sandy could see that her friend had become serious and attentive, so she reciprocated in kind as she related Nathan's experience with his dog. Leslie's face betrayed no emotion as she listened.

"So, Nathan believes that what he saw that day was a ghost," Leslie said.

"Yes."

"A murderous ghost."

"Yes. But there's more. I had an unsettling experience right here in the house." She went on to tell her about the presence she felt in the loft at the top of the stairs. Leslie glanced in that direction when Sandy mentioned the stairs. When she had finished telling her story, she said, "I'm not saying that what I experienced was a ghost, but it was very strange. Nathan believes it's a ghost."

"Two ghosts, then?"

"Yes, what Nathan called the Spirit Eater and this other unknown ghost."

Leslie was quiet. She seemed to be concentrating on something, lost in her own thoughts. Sandy did not know was wrong, but she did not intrude upon her friend's musings, knowing that Leslie would tell her what was on her mind when she was good and ready and not before. After a few moments, in a voice not much more than a whisper, she said, "It's incredible, but it must be true."

"Well, maybe it's true," Sandy said

Leslie shook her head. "No, I mean what my father had written in his journals. He talked about it later, but I never really believed him, thinking he was just telling stories. But now, I'm having second thoughts."

"What are you talking about?"

"My father's journals. You've seen them, right?"

"Yes, I have and I'm sorry if I was prying . . ."

She waved a hand. "No, forget it. Did you read them all?"

"I don't know. I read some."

"Come with me," she said, rising from the couch, "I want you to see something."

She led Sandy into the bedroom at the front of the house and opened the closet.

"I've already seen the gun." Leslie ignored her comment and pushed the box containing the gun to one side. Sandy heard her fingernails scratching at the wood at the rear of the closet, and then heard the wood creaking as Leslie pried loose a board in the back wall above the shelf. Sandy stepped closer but could not see what she was doing.

"Got it!" Leslie said, excitedly. She backed out of the closet clutching in one hand an old, leather-bound book. There were no words inscribed upon the spine or the cracked brown cover of the book. She sat on the bed, the book in her lap.

"In one of his journals my father had written that he had acquired a book, a diary actually, that pertained to the history of Dudleytown. He hid the book, this book," she said, holding it up for Sandy to see, "in the wall. I read it once after he died, and I understood why he had hidden it. But until tonight, I never believed what I read in the diary was true."

"What is it?" Sandy peered over her friend's shoulder.

"My father was curious about everything—you can see that from his journals—but he really liked history. He told me he had gone to an auction once, an estate sale, and bought a box of books cheap. In the bottom of the box, he found this book."

She carefully opened the book. Sandy saw the cream-colored pages were discolored deeper brown at the edges. The pages were faintly lined. Elegant handwriting in black ink now faded to gray gracefully flowed across the pages.

"This is a diary kept by a medical doctor named Harlan Richards," Leslie said. "Actually, he was more than a medical doctor. He was interested in mental illness and devoted his practice to that field. He wrote about some of his patients in this book."

"When was this?" Sandy said.

"Just after the Civil War. The entries span about four years, from 1864 to 1868. Doctor Richards worked at the Hartford Retreat for the Insane." She slowly turned the pages. "My father had no idea what he would find in the book. He was just his usual curious self. But then, he came across some entries that had a direct connection to Dudleytown. Here they are," she said, stopping midway through the book.

She handed the book to Sandy. "Read this. I think it will blow your mind." Sandy held the book carefully. "There are quite a few pages there, take your time."

The smooth, worn leather felt cool in her hands. She looked at the handwritten script on the pages. Could anything so beautiful really be all that horrible?

FIFTEEN

Sandy settled herself on the bed in the loft and began to read Doctor Richards' diary.

March 3, 1865
It had been rumored for some time that the Hartford Retreat would soon be in custody of Mrs., Constance Pruett, the notorious murderess who had spent the last three years in the state penitentiary and now came to us as what the officials there had deemed incurably insane. So, I had been forewarned and yet, the appearance of Mrs. Pruett at our facility created a flutter of excitement among the staff and, I will admit, within me as well. Perhaps, if the lurid details of her crime had not been so ballyhooed in the newspapers, she would have created not a ripple among us but alas, her infamy preceded her.

Small in stature and slight of build, Mrs. Pruett seemed incapable of even lifting an ax, let alone wielding one forcefully enough to hack to death her husband and two children. When I first saw her in her room, she was sitting in a chair, a flat affect upon her otherwise not uncomely face. She did not acknowledge my presence but merely continued to gaze out the window at the snowy drifts leading down to the river. She wore a long black dress and her dark hair was pinned up in braids that encircled her head like a wreath. In short, she appeared as a very proper woman that would be welcomed in any lady's sewing circle.

I addressed her by name and introduced myself, but she neither looked at me nor replied, keeping her attention focused upon the scene outside the barred window. I sat in a chair opposite her and waited. She kept her hands demurely folded on her lap and she seemed to me very much composed, not at all discomforted by finding herself in the asylum. Indeed, this place would be a welcomed change from the penitentiary, her former domicile. We sat quietly, she studying the leaden sky outside, and me studying her posture and countenance.

I am a man of patience, but Mrs. Pruett was equally patient. After about twenty minutes in which neither of us spoke, nor exchanged even a single glance, I rose from my chair and, informing Mrs. Pruett that I had other patients yet to visit, I told her I would be back to see her on the following day. At that moment, she finally turned her head to look at me and I saw such an expression of fear in her eyes that it brought me up short. Still, she would not speak and so I left, locking the door behind me.

March 12, 1865
I continued to visit Mrs. Pruett daily, but each day was much like the first. She would not speak to me, but merely sat in her chair, her eyes directed to the window and whatever it was she saw there that interested her so. When she would look at me, generally as I was leaving, I saw the fear still in her eyes. What she feared I did not know.

March 20, 1865
While my time was taken up by my other patients, several of them poor soldiers recently returned from the battlefield, their wits addled by the carnage of war, Mrs. Pruett's case weighed heavily upon my mind. My other patients all communicated with me in some manner; many of them spoke to me in civil conversation, a few ranted and raved incoherently, and one cursed me and hurled invectives at me, but Mrs. Pruett refused to speak

at all. Despite the fact that I visited her daily and tried to engage her in conversation, she remained stubbornly mute. Further, she would sit very still, almost as though she were catatonic, until the last moment when, with a birdlike motion, she would turn and look at me as I was about to leave, and those fearful eyes would shoot through me. Shakespeare said that the eyes are the windows to the soul and if that be true, Mrs. Pruett's soul is that of a trapped and terrified animal, to be approached with empathy, perhaps, but also a great deal of caution.

I do not make it a habit to discuss my patients with anyone outside the asylum, but my wife could see that I had been distracted since the arrival of Mrs. Pruett and it worried her. Poor Clarissa. It is not easy being a doctor's wife, but Clarissa bore her burden with grace and composure and had done so for almost twenty years. Still, she worried about me and, finally, I told her about Mrs. Pruett. Without giving her all the details of Mrs. Pruett's case—although Clarissa had read enough about the woman in the newspapers a few years back—I told her how unsuccessful I had been with my patient thus far and how I feared that I might not ever be able to reach her. Clarissa's touch and her kind words soothed me and gave me the confidence to try again—perhaps she should have been a doctor as well.

Sandy smiled as she read the entry. Poor Doctor Richards had been as confused and vexed by his patient as she was with Kevin. But at least Richards had a loving wife in whom he could confide, a wife that stood beside him, comforted him, and loved him without reservation. She could detect all that in the doctor's words. At one time she thought that Kevin could have given her the same love that Clarissa showed for her husband. How quickly, though, she discovered her error. Kevin was not like that and would never be.

She heard Leslie in the kitchen below and the rattle of pots. The loft was growing darker as the sun began to fade from the sky, so she switched on the light on the bedside table.

"Do you feel like dinner?" Leslie called up from the kitchen.

"In a few minutes. I want to read some more of the journal first," Sandy replied.

She turned back to Doctor Richards' journal.

April 10, 1865
What news! Yesterday, General Lee surrendered his army to General Grant at a place called Appomattox Court House. Only a week or so before we had received the glorious news that Richmond had fallen to federal forces; Harper's Weekly carried a wonderful engraving of President Lincoln entering the city in a landau carriage. We all feel buoyed with hope that the end of this long and bloody war is at last near at hand.

April 15, 1865
Telegraph wires all across the country, indeed, all around the world have carried the awful news and today's newspapers trumpet it in large characters— President Lincoln is dead, struck down by an assassin's bullet yesterday, Good Friday, in Washington. Only a few days after Lee's surrender when the end of the war was finally in sight. Now, with this tragic news, no one can be sure of anything.

How is it possible that our beloved President could be murdered? We all ask this question, that is when we are not so stunned that we can actually talk about it. There is a strange silence in the city and people go about with dazed expressions on their faces, unable to fathom the news, each of them silently asking, What do we do now? Everything has come to a halt; the businesses are all shuttered, no traffic moves in the streets, the schools are not open. The only gatherings are those held in churches and they are aplenty, with people asking God why He has allowed such an evil deed to befall us. God does not answer.

It was all I could do to muster the energy to visit my patients, but duty is duty. With a heavy heart I walked to the Retreat, nodding to the teary-eyed people I passed, finding in them a new connection created by our mutual grief. I spoke briefly with our handyman, Oscar Piper, as he shoveled from the walk the slush left by a spring thaw. Even though he is an Indian, a Golden Hill Paugussett from Bridgeport, he too, was saddened by the death of our chief.

I entered the building, hung my coat in my office, and proceeded to make the rounds of my patients. It seemed to me that I was only going through the motions as I spoke with them, that I could not give them my undivided attention and for that I was sorry. But it could not be helped.

I knocked on Mrs. Pruett's door to announce myself, then unlocked it and entered. As usual, she sat in her chair by the window. As usual, I took the chair opposite her. As usual, she did not speak to me; she did not look at me. After a few minutes of that, something inside me broke free and I suddenly felt angry toward Mrs. Pruett. Unreasonable, yes, but I was angry that she could sit there so dispassionately, so silently, when the world outside had just been turned upside down.

See here, Mrs., Pruett, I said, in a rather unkindly voice, you do know that President Lincoln has been murdered, don't you?

She blinked her eyes then slowly turned her face toward me. Our eyes met, and her lips parted. In a voice little more than a whisper she said, "It is nothing," and then turned back to the window.

I was speechless. Those were the first words she had ever spoken since she had come to us and, despite their inappropriateness, my heart jumped to hear her speak. I recovered my senses and tried to engage her in further conversation, but she would have none of it. Still, I left her room with hope in my bosom. She had spoken.

April 17, 1865
Mrs. Pruett began to speak to me, granted not much more than a sentence or two each day, but she was beginning to communicate and that was the important thing. Another man would have stopped trying altogether to get her to speak. To what end, after all? She was an insane murderess; why bother? It was more than my oath that urged me to continue working with her. I was fascinated by the fact that such an impassive, but refined and cultured woman could have committed a crime so heinous in nature. I wanted to know how. I wanted to know why.

Still rankled by her response to our martyred president's death, I continued to ask her what she meant by saying "It is nothing" and gradually came to understand that she had witnessed something so horrible that the murder of President Lincoln paled by comparison. She referred to the gruesome murders, I am sure, but there was something beyond the simple fact of them, a deeper horror that she had not revealed. It was evident in her eyes as she stared fearfully through the window as though awaiting some malevolent visitor. At such times, I wanted to comfort her but did not, wary of a gesture that might seem inappropriate and unprofessional. Truth be told, I questioned my own motives, wondering how much they were simple human empathy and how much an attraction to the person of Mrs. Pruett.

June 10, 1865
So much has happened with Mrs. Pruett over the last month or so that I have not had the time to record everything. It seems that I may have finally gained her trust for she will speak to me now more at length, although slowly and precisely, as though to make sure that each word she spoke was exactly the one she wanted and that her meaning would be crystal clear to me. And what she said completely astounded me. as she

told me that she was not the murderess of her husband
and children; she was innocent.

Certainly, I had heard former patients maintain their
innocence despite their obvious culpability, just as the
prisons are filled with innocent men, so my immediate
reaction was that she was simply denying her crime
as a way of protecting what was left of her humanity.
How could a woman murder her children? Deep within
her soul she asked herself this question and came up
wanting for an answer. So, the simple solution, simple
to a person not right in her mind, was to deny she had
committed the act at all, just as my children would
answer "nobody" when I asked them who had drawn
pencil sketches on the wall.

Yet, as much as logic told me that the woman was
in denial, there was an earnestness to her words and
such a profound look in her eyes, that I began to
wonder if there was not some shred of truth to what she
maintained to be true. Perhaps, her husband killed the
children and then she, in turn, killed him in an act of
self-defense. Could it be that a stranger killed all three?
Mrs. Pruett barely testified in her own behalf during
her trial and what she did say seemed like incoherent
nonsense. Now, with great emphasis, she maintained
her innocence.

It seems that Mrs. Pruett believed the murders
were committed by a ghost. Now I understood why she
had been released from the prison and sent to us at
the Retreat. No one in his right mind would believe in
ghosts, let alone blame one for murder. But when Mrs.
Pruett told me that, she looked at me with a level gaze,
her voice soft but confident. She was convinced that a
ghost had killed her family.

I thought it best to explore her fantasy, thinking that
by doing so I could eventually discover some chink in
her mental armor that would allow me to bring home
the truth of her crime to her. "Tell me about the ghost,"
I said.

She looked away, as though to hide from me the truth in her, focusing instead upon the bright spring greenery coming into bloom outside her window. I waited. Still looking away, she began to speak. I leaned forward to hear her.

"It was horrible," she said. "Monstrous; I was terrified." I noticed that her fingers worried a handkerchief on her lap as she spoke, balling it up and then smoothing it out repeatedly. "It filled the room with its presence."

"What did it look like?" I said.

"Green. A glowing green light."

I wasn't sure I had heard her correctly. "Green?"

She nodded her head almost imperceptibly. "An Indian." She turned her head to me and I saw that her eyes were wet with tears. "The Spirit Eater," she whispered. After that, she went silent, tears streaming from her eyes and would not speak further.

It was clear that she was distraught, so I did not push her. Before I left the Retreat, I ordered the matron to give Mrs. Pruett some laudanum to calm her nerves and help her sleep.

As I walked back home, the sweet fragrance of a New England spring surrounded me while birds, newly returned from warmer southern climes, called to me cheerfully and I marveled, as I always did, at how remarkable the real world was and how incredibly different from the many bizarre worlds inhabited by my patients. Mrs. Pruett could stare out her window for hours on end, but I sincerely doubted that she saw God's beautiful creation. Most likely for her, it was all darkness and horror, evil and fear. It would be a miracle, indeed, if I could help her see through that darkness

I sat in my study late that night, thinking over Mrs. Pruett's words. Her wild imaginings posited not only a ghost, but an Indian ghost, and a tall, green Indian ghost to boot. Where would she have come up with that phantasm? A credit to the insane mind, I suppose, that such fanciful creations abound. Perhaps that explains the common perception that so many artists are at least in part, mad.

June 11, 1865
This day was as lovely as the previous one and I enjoyed my leisurely walk to the Retreat. As I drew near to the asylum I noticed the brown figure of Oscar Piper busily pulling up weeds from the flower beds that graced the front lawn. Piper was an affable enough man and would greet me as I passed by, but we did not often exchange more than a few "good-mornings" to each other. Today, though, as I admired the newly blossomed flowers, I stopped and complimented Oscar upon the excellent job he was doing keeping the grounds so neatly groomed. He smiled shyly and thanked me. We spoke a bit more about the flowers and then, for whatever reason, I felt compelled to ask him if he had ever heard of something called a Spirit Eater.

Oscar's countenance grew even darker than his natural nut-brow color. "Why do you ask?" he said.

Of course, I could not reveal to him any of my conversations with Mrs. Pruett so I made up a story and told him that I had been reading a history book about Indians and came across the reference to the Spirit Eater and thought that, him being an Indian, he might know something about it and could enlighten me.

"I'm Paugussett, Doctor Richards," Oscar said. There was a tone in his voice that I did not recognize, but I simply nodded my head.

"Have you ever heard of the Spirit Eater?" I persisted.

Oscar sighed, as though I had just asked him to clear another hundred flower beds. He looked at me, his dark eyes serious. "Yes, I know of him, but we do not often talk of him," he said. He paused for a few moments and I was about to prod him to continue when he spoke. "My people know him from long ago, in the Beginning Times. When Creator make good, he also make evil, so that there would be balance in the world. All that is evil is the Spirit Eater."

"How did he get his name?" I asked.

"A man who falls into evil ways and does not repent is cursed. He becomes one with the Spirit Eater who eats the man's spirit. The poor man is caught, banned from entering the happy place where his ancestors dwell."

"So, it's like hell," I said.

Oscar shrugged. "Maybe, in some ways," he said. "You might think of the Spirit Eater as the devil, although he is much more than that."

"And you say your people knew this creature from long ago?"

"Yes," said Oscar, "but he is still with us today, the people say. One of our heroes defeated the Spirit Eater long ago, banishing him from our world, but a sachem called him back."

"Why?" I asked.

"To curse them white men who murdered him. He made the curse with his dying words."

"And can this Spirit Eater be defeated?" I asked, and it occurred to me as I asked that question that I was giving too much credence to Mrs. Pruett's fevered imagination."

"A child," Oscar said.

"What do you mean?"

"They say a child, innocent and pure in heart, can defeat it," he replied.

I thought about all that Oscar had told me. It was a fantastic tale, but no more or less fantastic than the ancient Greek legends I had been taught as a child.

"Is that all a legend or do your people actually believe in the Spirit Eater?" I asked.

Oscar said, "Is the devil a legend, or do your people actually believe in him?"

Touché, I thought.

There were more of Doctor Richards' entries that Sandy wanted to read, but she felt her eyes growing heavy. She closed the journal and set it on the table beside the bed. Tomorrow she would finish his story.

She opened her eyes. The loft was dark. She glanced at the clock by the bed; two AM. She didn't know what had awakened her, but she was wide awake. The house was quiet. Leslie must be asleep, she thought. She remembered Leslie asking her about dinner, but she did not go downstairs to eat. She must have dozed off right after that.

She lay on her back, looking up through the skylight. There was no moon that night, the skylight gaping like a black hole into another dimension. She closed her eyes again, hoping that sleep would find her, but her brain refused to doze, and she found herself thinking about Dr. Richards' journal. No use fighting it, she thought, she was awake anyway. She switched on the bedside lamp and picked up the leather-bound journal. Propping up her pillows, she settled herself with the book and began to read.

> June 15, 1865
> Now that all Confederate forces have finally surrendered, and our long national nightmare come to an end, all citizens of our restored country, both North and South, are wondering what happens next. So many dead and maimed, so much property destroyed, so much rancor still seething among large portions of our citizenry. Our beloved President Lincoln had once made a speech in which he called for "malice toward none, with charity for all." Will his words become prophetic for how our country will bind itself together, or will men of lesser stature than Lincoln balk at his words? It remains to be seen of what stuff we Americans are truly composed.
>
> The end of the war, though, does not affect my doctoring of Mrs. Pruett. Though she has become more voluble, her situation, for the most part, remains unchanged. I had asked her to elaborate upon the Spirit Eater since I was intrigued by Oscar Piper's stories and wondered how a woman like Mrs. Pruett came to know of them. As near as I could determine she was no

authority on Indian legends and probably did not know any Indians, yet, what she said about the Spirit Eater matched Oscar Piper's information. Could she simply have imagined such a creature after, perhaps, hearing bits and pieces of Indian lore over the years? Was that possible? Connecticut was full of places named after Indians and it would not be impossible for one living here to pick up tidbits of Indian lore, even if accidentally.

This morning when I visited Mrs. Pruett in her room I found her, as usual, sitting in her chair near the barred window. I was surprised to see that she was not wearing her customary black garb but was instead clothed in a summery white muslin dress. She looked as though she was prepared to go on a picnic and I was encouraged to see her so, thinking that her depression was lifting. The bright light streaming through the window struck gleaming highlights in her dark hair and, playing upon the white fabric of her dress, revealed the contours of her figure in ways that her former black dress had not. I realized that my attention was drifting and so brought my eyes directly back to hers as I drew up a chair across from her.

Despite her gay apparel, Mrs. Pruett's eyes did not radiate anything other than the sadness and fear I had always seen in them. But she did not turn from me as she so often had done, keeping her gaze leveled on mine.

"I saw him," she said, almost as soon as I had sat down.

"Saw him?" I said. "Who are you talking about?"

"Spirit Eater," she said.

She went on to say that she had seen the ghost—that was her word for it—in a dream the night before. When I pressed her, she described it as a tall, powerful Indian that seemed to glow. She said that he carried a war club and that little lights like fireflies flickered inside his figure.

I explained to her that, yes, she was correct, it was a dream and nothing to fear, except that she did fear it and nothing I could say allayed those fears. She suddenly leaned forward and snatched up my hand. We had never made any kind of physical contact before and her warm hand squeezing mine so urgently was like an electric jolt through my body. Her eyes bored into mine.

"He's coming for me," she whispered.

I sat there for a moment, shocked by her words and momentarily flustered by the intimacy of her hand grasping mine. But she did not let go and I did not withdraw my hand. I found my voice at last and reminded her that it was only a dream.

"Dreams can't hurt you," I said.

She looked at me and I saw a shift in the set of her lips, almost a rueful smile, but not quite. "Can't they?" she said. Then, she released my hand and sat back in her chair.

After that, she went silent. I sat there for a few minutes more, hoping that she would have more to say, but to no avail. I replaced the chair in the corner, bid her adieu and left her room.

As I walked back to my home I thought about her dream—her nightmare—and what it might signify for her. I am convinced that dreams contain some meaning, some guidance for our lives if we only knew how to interpret them, and I labored to find something useful in Mrs. Pruett's dream. Of course, I did not know if the dreams of the insane were as fanciful as their waking moments or whether they too, could be as insightful for them as they would be for any sane person. After all, Thoreau said, "Dreams are the touchstones of our character." I believe that to be true.

So, I pondered Mrs. Pruett's dream as I found my way home, but even more, I found myself remembering the touch of her hand in mine.

June 18, 1865

Mrs. Pruett told me that she had dreamed again of the Spirit Eater last night. In fact, she said that she had dreamed of him for the last four nights. While it is not unusual for dreams to repeat over a period of time, it did seem odd to me that the exact same dream—as Mrs. Pruett claimed—would visit her on four consecutive nights. The poor woman was terrified.

"He is coming for me!" she said, whispering the words urgently, both her hands tightly gripping mine.

I tried to console her as best I could, reminding her that it was only a dream, frightening, yes, but a dream just the same. I reached over and rapped on the iron bars across the window. "See?" I said. "This iron is real, it's solid, not a dream. You are perfectly safe here. You need only to banish your nightmares from your mind."

She laughed derisively, the first time I had ever heard her laugh. "You don't know," she said. Her eyes were frantic. "Useless," she said, shaking her head and I didn't know if she was referring to the ironwork or to me. She released my hands and sat back in her chair, an expression of sad resignation written across her face.

"You won't help me," she said, accusingly.

Perhaps, I thought, I was taking the wrong tack with her. No matter what I thought about her nightmares, they were real to her. Maybe I should indulge her paranoia. "Alright," I said, gently, "let me see if I can help you. Tell me why you believe the Spirit Eater is coming for you."

She looked at me for a moment, as though testing my sincerity, then spoke. "Because I know."

"Know what?"

"I know it murdered my family," she said.

Ah, that old excuse again, I thought. How would I ever dissuade her of that belief? Follow her lead, see where it takes me, I thought. "That was a few years ago, Mrs. Pruett. Why do you think he's coming for you now, after so long? Why didn't he come before?"

"Because I never spoke about him before," she said. "He's afraid now."

"Come now. A monster of a ghost is afraid? That's hard to believe, wouldn't you agree?"

She spoke to me as if I was a child, simply and patiently, trying to make herself understood. "No one knew about him before. Now you know. And now that you know, he's afraid that you will destroy him."

"So, he's coming for you?" I asked. She nodded her head. "Revenge? But if he's afraid I will destroy him, why doesn't he come for me instead?"

She looked into my eyes. "He will, Doctor," she said, softly. "He will."

June 19, 1865
I am stunned. Mrs. Pruett is dead.

That brief entry startled her, the words hitting her like a slap in the face. Doctor Richards' entries had seemed like a novel to her with Mrs. Pruett the heroine and Sandy had not expected her to die. But death was everywhere a character in the history of Dudleytown. What was one more? She read on.

June 20, 1865
It was all I could do to write those brief lines yesterday, consumed as I was by the facts of her death and my medical obligations toward my deceased patient. Just a little after dawn yesterday morning Oscar Piper came to my door, pounding on it excitedly, saying that I was urgently needed at the asylum. I dressed quickly and hurried out.

Oscar waited for me on the porch, lantern in hand, but refused to answer my questions, feigning ignorance of the situation that was soon to reveal itself to me. When we arrived at the Retreat the matron, Mrs. Warren, stood in the foyer wringing her hands, tears in her eyes.

"It's Mrs. Pruett," she said, and I bolted up the stairs, the matron and Oscar close behind.

The door to her room was ajar. I pushed it completely open. The early morning light was coming in through the window, but it was partially blocked by what seemed to be a white ghost floating in the air, but as my eyes adjusted to the light I saw that the ghost was Mrs. Pruett, hanging by the neck from the iron bars over the window.

I heard Mrs. Warren sobbing behind me. Oscar cursed softly under his breath. I stood there as though made of marble as my eyes took in the details of the grisly scene before me. I can't bear to write down what I saw and will suffice it to say only that no one should ever have to gaze upon the face of a hanged person. It is a memory that will remain with me forever.

At last I was able to tear my eyes away. I turned to the matron and closed the door behind me. "Tell me what happened," I said.

The matron dabbed at her eyes with a handkerchief and composed herself. "I don't rightly know, Doctor," she said. "No one heard anything unusual but when we made our bed checks in the morning there she was, hanging there. I don't know when she did it."

"Alright," I said. Turning to the groundskeeper I said, "Oscar, you get a couple of the other men and get her down from there. Place her in the examination room." He nodded and went off to gather his crew.

I dismissed Mrs. Warren and shut myself in my office. It was always difficult to lose a patient, especially when death came unexpectedly. I sat at my desk, the morning light now streaming brightly into the room through the tall mullioned windows, doing nothing to cheer my depression. Suicide. How did I not see the signs? But what had brought her to that point? She had already served a few years in the penitentiary and had never tried to take her life there. And here, at the Retreat, she seemed to be gradually responding to me. Did I simply underestimate the fear I saw in her eyes? In our last conversation, she had said that she feared for her life— and that mine was in jeopardy as well—as the Spirit Eater feared us. A ridiculous notion, of course, but was that enough to drive her to suicide? What could I have done differently? How could I have saved her?

A rap on my door interrupted my musings. It was Oscar. He told me that Mrs. Pruett's body was now in the examination room, but that there was something very strange about it.

I proceeded to the examination room and entered to find Mrs. Pruett in her white dress lying supine on the table. I saw that someone had mercifully placed a white cloth over her disfigured face, but what I saw immediately—and had missed as she hung in the bright window—was that the poor woman's hands were tied behind her back!

How could she have hanged herself with her hands tied? Her death was no suicide; it was murder.

June 25, 1865

The police have been investigating Mrs. Pruett's death for the last several days but have come up with nothing to substantiate the fact that she was murdered, despite the curious fact of how she was found. According to their report thus far, the door to Mrs. Pruett's room was locked and had not been opened during the night when she died. It wasn't until the morning bed check that a matron unlocked the door and by then Mrs. Pruett was already dead. The window had not been tampered with and the iron bars remained intact. The police have identified no motive for killing her nor have they identified anyone as a suspect in the crime; they even interrogated me extensively.

The coroner supports hanging as the cause of death but, in light of the lack of evidence to the contrary, considers her death a suicide. The police say that she used the sash from her dress to fashion a noose, stood on the chair to attach it to the window, and then kicked the chair away.

With her hands tied behind her back.

The police maintain that she could have tied the noose to the window first, before tying her hands behind her, and then kicked away the chair. I can't imagine that is what happened. I was in possession of the cord—an old-fashioned looking braided cord—that had encircled Mrs. Pruett's wrists and I tried myself to tie my hands together behind me. It was impossible. How could she have done so? A circus contortionist could not have succeeded in that endeavor.

I believe Mrs. Pruett was murdered. I have no idea who may have committed the act, but I am reluctant to believe in a murderous ghost. I cannot let my mind dwell on such a preposterous notion.

June 26, 1865

This morning I sat in my office, the door open, filling out the legal forms demanded by the state upon the death of a patient. Since the police had closed the case, satisfied that, as bizarre as it seemed, Mrs. Pruett had taken her own life, so there was no reason for me to delay any longer. Now, the poor woman could be buried in the Retreat cemetery where, God willing, she would finally find peace. A shadow fell across the desk and I looked up to find Oscar Piper standing in the doorway, his soiled cap in his hands. I don't know how long he had been standing there.

"Excuse me, Doctor," he said. "I wanted to let you know that the grave is dug."

"Thank you, Oscar," I said. He nodded but didn't move. "Is there something else?"

He stood there, eyeing something on my desk. "That there cord," he said, "might I take a gander at it?"

I handed him the cord that had been removed from Mrs. Pruett's body. He turned it over in his hands, inspecting it closely. "This came off Mrs. Pruett?" he said.

"Yes."

"It's Indian work, you know," Oscar said, handing the cord back to me.

"Indian?" I said.

"I seen this kind of braid when I was a boy. Notice them green fibers in it? They's from a plant the Indians used. Not no more, though," Oscar said.

"What do you mean?"

"That there cord's old, Doctor Richards. Them plants don't grow here no more. That's an antique you got there," he said.

After Oscar left I sat there deep in thought. Whoever murdered Mrs. Pruett—and I insist that it was murder—tied her hands with a cord made by an Indian. The only Indian here was Oscar and there was no way that he was complicit in her murder. So, who then? Am I really to believe that she was murdered by an Indian ghost?

SIXTEEN

What was she to make of such a story? Sandy closed the journal and set it upon the bedside table. She rolled onto her back and lay there looking up to where dawn was slowly coloring in the patch of sky framed by the skylight. Doctor Richards had been a man of science, a logical, rational man, but he had been rattled by something he could not explain in any way that made sense. He was certain that Mrs. Pruett had been murdered. The problem was that no murderer could be found, at least no human murderer.

Did she believe that a ghost had killed the woman? She found it unnerving that Spirit Eater, the ghost Nathan had first told her about, was a central character in the journal written more than a century and a half ago. Worse, the ghost was a prime suspect in Mrs. Pruett's death. Still, it was impossible to believe some green ghost slithered in through the barred windows of the asylum, tied up its victim, and hung her in the window like a macabre sun-catcher. She would have to be really, really drunk before she would believe such a story.

But then, how do I explain Nathan's encounter with the ghost? Nathan was not a crazy man and when he first told her about his lost dog and seeing the ghost in the woods, there was conviction in his voice. He was certain of what he had seen. She believed him then; did she still?

She sighed. The sky above was light. She heard sounds downstairs—Leslie in the kitchen—and she suddenly felt hungry, no surprise since she had slept through dinner the evening before. She rolled out of bed and threw on some clothes.

"I guess you slept well," Leslie said, as Sandy entered the kitchen. "When you didn't come down for dinner, I thought I should go up and wake you, but then I thought better of it."

"Sorry about that." She pulled out a chair. "That journal mesmerized me. I read it until I fell asleep and then woke up in the middle of the night to finish it."

Leslie leaned against the counter, a cup of coffee in her hand. "I knew you'd find it interesting. What do you think? Were all those people crazy or was there a ghost?"

She shook her head. "I don't know what to make of it, Les."

Leslie sipped her coffee, then placed the mug on the counter. "My father believed the story."

"He did?"

"Yes, especially when he did some more research on Doctor Richards. It seems that only two years after the death of Mrs. Pruett the good doctor killed himself."

"Jesus," Sandy said, softly. "Let me guess. . . "

Leslie nodded her head. "That's right, he hanged himself."

After a while, she said, "That still doesn't mean there was a ghost."

"No, it doesn't."

"Les, you know that I'm open to a lot of ideas. I don't know what happens after we die. I don't buy the idea of heaven or hell but I'm open to the possibility that we go on in some way. Maybe somewhere along the line, somewhere between here and there—wherever there is—some of us get lost, get off the bus one stop short of our destination. Maybe that's what a ghost is, I don't know. But it's hard to believe that such a being could murder living people. That's a big leap for me to make. No, I'm more afraid of the living psychos out there, Kevin for example."

"Yes, of course," Leslie said. "I'm with you on that and we have to remember that Kevin *is* out there somewhere. He's no ghost."

"Right, but he *is* dangerous."

Kevin was still at large, no doubt still intent upon getting Sandy back, or worse, paying Sandy back and that troubled Nathan. All he knew about the man was what the women had told him but that was enough to make him believe the man was not merely dangerous, he was deranged. A terrifying combination. He had seen some men like that—blessedly, only a few—in Iraq. They fought with a tenacity and fury that went far beyond duty and valor. They fought as though they got off on the killing and bloodshed, the smell of cordite and blood aphrodisiacs to those whacked-out killers. Their uniforms gave them license for their ferociousness and their atrocities, but what happened to them when they returned home and hung up their uniforms for the last time? He had heard stories of some of the men he knew in Iraq coming to bad ends, very bad ends, after returning stateside. He shuddered to think that Kevin could be like those men. Perhaps, not a veteran, but psychotic nonetheless, the kind of guy who grew up stuffing firecrackers down the throats of frogs. That kind of guy.

The women's decision to stay at the house instead of coming into town was a bad idea. He was certain of that, yet he could not convince them otherwise. He had to admire their courage, but it seemed bravery born out of stubbornness and that was not always enough. If Kevin was out there scouting the house, watching them, he would make his move soon, Nathan was sure. Did the women have any clue?

That was why he was making it a point to stay close to the house, to run his own patrols since the police were looking elsewhere if they were looking for Kevin at all. The women didn't have to know what he was doing, although he did believe they would appreciate his looking out for them, even if they thought they could manage on their own. He was no hero, though. Dark Entry—Dudleytown—scared him and it wasn't only because of Kevin. Whether Sandy believed him or not, he knew what he had seen that day in the deep woods and he did not want to see it again.

Sweet-Boy wandered in the woods now, afraid to return to his shack in the ravine. Spirit Eater was back, an evil force that must be avoided at all cost. As long as he remained on the move, never lingering too long in any one spot, he could keep away from that awful spirit. He had been successful so far and that was the way he wanted to keep it.

With the memories that had been suddenly flooding through him he knew that Spirit Eater was a killer. It was responsible for the deaths of his parents and so many others. Spirit Eater had killed him, he was certain, if not directly, then by forcing him into the woods where he could not survive. The little memorial that bore his name, standing forlornly in the woods, was proof of the entity's guilt. Yet, despite his fear of Spirit Eater—and that fear was strong—he was aware of a spark taking hold inside him. In that burning ember were the faces of all those that Spirit Eater had claimed over the years. He could see them clearly, each one of them. He could hear their voices crying out to him, begging him to help them, to free them. Their pitiful cries echoing in his head stoked his anger against Spirit Eater. What could he do, though, against such a powerful force? Even if he could find the courage to face the spirit, where would he ever find the strength to defeat it? He was just a boy. Maybe it was just better to shut his ears against the urgent whisperings of those lost souls and save his own skin. What else could a poor ghost do?

What remained of Kevin lay in the woods, bloodied and torn to shreds. Nathan felt the bile rise within him as he stood there looking down at the mutilated corpse lying in an old cellar hole. Nothing he had ever seen in Iraq had prepared him for the grisly sight. It was evident that animals had been at work on the corpse, but the complete desecration of the body could not have been the work of animals. The psychos he had known from his time in the military? Yes. But animals? No. He felt his stomach heave and he turned away from the body before he almost lost his breakfast.

He would have to call the police, and of course, tell Sandy what he had discovered. But what he had discovered was even worse news than the simple fact of Kevin's death. The man should not be dead. The police had been looking for *him*, fearing that he would come after Sandy, but now he was very much dead himself. Whoever had killed him was clearly more dangerous and deranged than anyone had imagined.

He turned away from the body and walked back up the hillside to his truck, pushing through the dense bushes impeding his path. Who had killed Kevin? He remembered the horrible vision of the ghost the day his dog had been killed, but despite that incident, it was difficult for him to think that a ghost—even one as fearsome as the legendary Spirit Eater—could have killed Kevin.

He sat in the truck and called the state police officer that had been in charge of the investigation. He checked the GPS system in the truck and gave the officer the coordinates for his location before driving to Leslie's house.

Sandy's reaction to the grim news was as he expected. Shocked at first, the tears came later, Leslie doing her best to comfort her friend. Nathan understood that no matter what Kevin had become in the end he and Sandy had shared a life together. She would mourn the loss of that relationship, perhaps more than she mourned the loss of the man himself. He stood quietly watching as Leslie sat with Sandy, her arm around her, Sandy crying softly into her friend's shoulder. He thought that he would like to be able to comfort her in the same way, although that would be inappropriate. Leslie gave him a look that told him she had everything under control. There wasn't anything more he could do there, and the police would want to talk with him about his discovery, so he drove back down the road to where the cruisers were parked by the hillside.

There were several police cars lining the road, along with a white van. He got out of the truck and walked to the steep slope. Looking down, he saw a knot of officers laboring to haul a black body bag up the hillside. It probably didn't weigh all that much, he thought since there wasn't much left of the man, but the incline was steep and thick with weeds and briars; slow going. Trooper Larsen, the officer who had coordinated the previous search for Kevin, stood by his cruiser watching the men climb up the hill.

Larsen noticed Nathan and walked over to him. "Thanks for calling it in," he said. "We're not entirely sure that we've got our boy—the coroner will determine that—but the shreds of clothing that we found seem to match the clothes he was wearing when he disappeared, so I'm reasonably certain it's him."

Nathan nodded. "Good. What do you think happened?"

"Hard to say just yet." The trooper glanced down the slope where the men were nearing the top. "But I'm thinking he died of natural causes, maybe suicide."

"Really? Did you get a good look at him?"

"Animals."

"You don't think he was murdered?"

"My eighteen years on the force tell me not to rule anything out, but murder seems unlikely, don't you think? We were looking for him, but I don't have any reason to think that anyone else was doing the same. Is there something you know? Do you think he was murdered?" Larsen asked.

Nathan shook his head. "I don't know."

"The only person with a motive that we know of is Miss Lawrence and, frankly, I'm not betting on her."

"No, that's impossible. She could never do such a thing."

Larsen nodded. "Guess they're ready," he said, looking over at the team that was now carrying the body bag to the back of the van. "There are a few more guys from forensics working the scene down there, so I don't want you or anyone else wandering around messing it up."

"Understood."

"I'll let you all know what the coroner says once he's finished."

"Thanks, I appreciate that."

He caught a glimpse of the black bag just as one of the officers shut the van doors. Larsen climbed into his cruiser and followed the van down the road. The other cars followed, leaving only the two cars of the forensics team still collecting evidence at the scene.

He stood there watching the men working in the woods below him. Sunlight found its way through the quiet forest, illuminating a patch of road and warming the back of his neck. Around him, the evergreens and hemlocks stood tall as soldiers. The fragrance of pine and honeysuckle floated to him on a gentle breeze. The voices of the men beneath the hill were muffled in the deep woods and sounded to him far-off and dreamlike. Were it not for the men collecting bits of gore and bone from the site below, the whole scene would seem like a tranquil and peaceful dream.

The cry of a mournful owl, invisible in the woods, broke the crystalline silence, drawing his attention back to the men working at the crime scene. Any notion he had had of the place as a sweet dream transformed into a real nightmare with the recollection of Kevin's eviscerated and mangled body. Blood spattered the rocks and dripped from the weeds, pooling into the earth. Bones littered the ground, a few of the larger ones snapped in two like toothpicks. The jaw bone lay among shreds of black cloth, but the rest of the skull was missing.

If Kevin had killed himself and his body had never been found, then animals and the elements would have worked on the body, gradually rendering it to atoms, but that would have taken many months, perhaps years. The police had only been looking for him a few days before Nathan found his remains. There was simply not enough time for nature to have arranged such a grisly display. No, there was no way the man had killed himself.

The forensics team had finished its work. The men packed up their gear and trudged up the hillside to the cars, leaving a loopy river of yellow crime scene tape flowing through the woods. Nathan got into his truck as the men stowed their cases in the trunks of the cars. As the cars slowly drove away and down the mountain he headed back to Leslie's house.

She answered the door at his knock. Peering over her shoulder he could see she was alone.

"She's upstairs." Leslie tipped her head in the direction of the stairs. "Sleeping, I hope. Come in, Nathan."

"How's she doing?" he asked, as he entered the house.

Leslie shrugged. "As good as can be expected, I suppose. This is pretty shocking news, don't you think?"

"Yes, of course. God, she's had a rough time."

"Yes, but she'll get through it in time. At least now we know that she's safe. He can't hurt her anymore."

"No."

She sat in one of the chairs at the kitchen table and gestured for him to sit. She watched him slowly pull the chair out as though the act required all his concentration. "What is it, Nathan? Is something on your mind?"

He didn't want to alarm her, but he could see no way to sugar-coat his misgivings. "I'm not sure that she's out of danger. Or maybe any of us for that matter."

"What do you mean? Kevin was a threat and now he's gone. And good riddance, I say."

"Yes, he's gone but, Leslie, I found his remains and I'd bet my life on it that he did not kill himself."

She leaned forward in her chair. "What? If he didn't kill himself, then that leaves death by accident, natural causes, or murder. Right?" He nodded. "And you think it's murder, don't you?"

"Yes." She bit her lower lip and he saw that her hands had balled into fists. "Natural causes seem unlikely for a young and healthy guy . . ."

"But he used drugs."

"Okay, I suppose he could have O.D.'d on something, but I just don't think that's what happened, and I think an accident is also as unlikely. Not that he couldn't have had some kind of accident in the woods. I mean, the guy was a city boy, but the condition of the body makes me think accidental death is out of the question."

"Condition of the body?"

"Don't ask. You don't want to know," he said. "Just trust me on this one."

They were silent for a few moments, sitting there simply looking at each other, trying to comprehend the implications for them of Kevin's death.

"Murdered," she said, softly. She looked up at him. "Who?"

"That's the question, isn't it? Who killed Kevin? More importantly, is that person also after Sandy for some reason?"

"Christ. What did the police say?"

"Nothing much. They had a forensics team working at the site. We might learn more later, but it doesn't really matter. We need to be careful. We need to keep her safe."

"Yes." She slumped in her chair. "And maybe ourselves as well."

"What do you know about Kevin? Maybe we can figure out what to do if we had more information."

"I never liked him," she said, "from the first day I met him. He was arrogant, full of himself. Plus, I didn't trust him. I'm sure he had other women and Sandy knew it, too, whether or not she wanted to believe it."

"What about the drugs?"

"Sandy would know more about that than me, but I do know that he liked his coke. I don't think that he was involved in selling drugs if that's what you're asking. I think he was only a user, a party guy."

"Maybe he was in the business and he screwed someone over. That could be reason enough to kill him."

"I just don't know, Nathan. I tried to have as little to do with him as possible, so I don't know much about his friends or the company he kept. Even though it pained me to do so I tried to bite my tongue and not harangue Sandy with my opinions of him, at least until the time when he hit her. Then I told her exactly how I felt about him."

"It doesn't seem like we have much to go on. All we can do is keep our guard up and hope that the police come up with something."

"Yes."

"But Leslie, maybe it's about time you two came down into the village?"

Before she could answer, they heard Sandy coming down the stairs.

SEVENTEEN

It was obvious she had not slept well. Her hair was tangled. Her eyes were dull and listless, the skin around them puffy, and her lips were set in a tight line that made her seen sullen and grim. Still, he thought her beautiful.

She shuffled to the table and sat down. Leslie and Nathan were silent, unable to find words of comfort as they looked at her face so full of sorrow. "This is hard," she finally said.

"Oh, Sandy," said Leslie.

She kept her eyes focused downward on the placemat before her. A part of her brain idly recognized its colorful pattern as Mayan. Mayan, up here in Connecticut, how odd, she thought. Was that Leslie talking to her?

"Sandy," she was saying, "look at me. Sandy."

Nathan watched her closely. She sat there unmoving, only vaguely responsive. He had seen such emotional distress before in Iraq and he knew how dangerous it could be. A person could easily become unhinged by traumatic events. Each person's response was different, but depression was common and, God forbid, so was suicide. Instinctively, he reached across the table and clasped her hand.

"It's alright, Sandy," he said gently, "we're here for you." He continued to hold her hand and thought that he felt her softly squeeze his fingers.

"So hard," she repeated. She lifted her eyes to him. "What am I to do?"

The pitiful tone of her voice cut through him. "It's okay, there's nothing for you to do. Don't worry." Keeping his eyes on her, he leaned toward Leslie. He lowered his voice and asked her to call a doctor. "You know Albert Rizzoli, right?"

Leslie nodded. "He's a good friend. He'll come up here if you call him."

Leslie went into her bedroom to call the doctor. Nathan was dismayed by the lifelessness he saw in Sandy's eyes. Unconsciously, he squeezed her hand tighter as though he was pulling her back from the brink of something, and maybe he was.

"It's all my fault," she said, shaking her head. "I'm to blame."

"What do you mean? What's your fault?"

Her face twisted, and tears appeared in her eyes. "Kevin," she said. "It's my fault that he's dead."

"Sandy, no! Of course, it's not your fault."

She sniffled. "Yes, it is. I killed him." She sobbed, and the tears began to flow.

He got up and came around to where she sat at the table. Kneeling beside her, he put his arms around her. She leaned her head against his shoulder and cried. "Shhh, don't talk like that," he said, holding her tight.

"No, it's true. I killed him. I should have talked things out with him instead of . . . instead of sending him away like that."

"He was dangerous, Sandy. Crazy."

"Maybe, but we were a couple. I owed him that."

He looked up and saw Leslie standing in the doorway. She nodded silently to him and he understood that Doctor Rizzoli was on his way.

"If I had talked with him, he would have . . . would have . . ."

"What? Changed his ways? Become someone he wasn't?" His words sounded harsh, but he couldn't help it. If she had been his he would have given her anything she wanted, yet here she was, defending that piece of shit and making herself out as the bad guy again.

"Sandy, the guy had beaten you once before and damn near killed you only a few days ago. He was scum. You know that. There is no way in hell that you have any responsibility for what happened to him." Why couldn't she see that?

She did not speak any further but settled into the security of his embrace. She sobbed a little longer, but he felt her body begin to relax in his arms and he hoped that perhaps she was falling asleep. He thought that she must be exhausted. He didn't know how long he had held her, nor did he hear anyone at the door, but suddenly, Leslie and the doctor were both standing in the kitchen.

"Let's get her over to the couch," Doctor Rizzoli said.

Nathan and the doctor maneuvered Sandy to the couch and set her upon it, Leslie adjusting a pillow beneath her head. She opened her eyes now and then but, for the most part, she was asleep.

Rizzoli sat on the edge of the couch and checked her vital signs. He pried open her eyelids to shine a light into her eyes. "I'd like to talk with her when she's awake and alert, but for now, I'm going to give her a sedative to make sure she gets some sleep," the doctor said, opening his bag. He removed a syringe and injected it into her arm. Her brows knit together when the needle went in, but after that, she relaxed and lay peacefully on the couch.

"Thanks for coming out, Albert," Nathan said.

"No problem. How about filling me in about what's going on?" Nathan and Leslie related the events of the last few days to the doctor. "Good lord, you've all been through a lot. And now the police are looking for the murderer I assume?"

"They're not sure it's murder, yet," Nathan said.

"I see," said the doctor. "In any case, she seems to have been affected seriously by all this."

Nathan nodded. "Post-traumatic stress disorder?"

"Possibly," the doctor answered, "but, as I said, I'd like to talk with her when she's able."

"What do we do in the meantime, Albert?" Nathan asked.

"Just let her sleep. That's best for now. I'm thinking that I may have to put her on some anti-depressants. but I won't know for sure until I do a full work-up on her."

"Will she be alright?" Leslie asked.

"She'll sleep for a while, then I'll want to see her again"

"What about suicide?" Nathan said.

"Suicide? Are you crazy?" Leslie said. "She would never do such a thing."

"Listen," Nathan said gently, "you of all people should know that even the people we think are the least capable of such an act may go ahead and do it anyway."

"He's right," the doctor said. "I'm not saying that your friend is suicidal; I don't have enough information at this point to make such an assessment. Still, pay attention to her actions and especially to what she says. Suicides often talk about killing themselves before they actually do it."

"We'll watch her," Leslie said.

"Just let me know when she's awake and I'll come back out," Rizzoli said,

"Thanks, Albert," said Nathan, shaking the doctor's hand. "He's a good man," he said to Leslie after the doctor had left. "We've been friends a long time. He'll take good care of her."

Post-traumatic stress disorder? That diagnosis was being used way too often, Doctor Rizzoli thought as he nosed the silver Lexus down Dark Entry Road. That might be the correct diagnosis in the woman's case, but he wasn't about to jump to any conclusions until he had the time to do a complete work-up on her. But, Jesus, what was happening up here on the mountain? Like most people who lived on the plain below, Coltsfoot Mountain was a mystery to him, a place that inspired superstition and tall tales—not that he believed them, being a man of science—but also a place that most people simply ignored since no one except Leslie lived up there anymore. Was it really possible that a murderer was on the loose on the mountain? That seemed far-fetched, but Nathan believed it and Albert had always trusted his friend.

It was twilight when Rizzoli had arrived at Leslie's house and now the deepening shadows of dusk surrounded his car. The bumpy road ahead was like a dark hole through which he descended, the headlights on the Lexus as effective as fireflies. He could not remember the last time he had been on that road and he drove slowly, careful not to miss a turn. In several places, there was no shoulder and no guard-rails existed anywhere to protect him from driving off into the darkness below. The road was steep, causing him to hit the brakes constantly.

It was no wonder that Nathan had thought of post-trau-matic stress disorder, Rizzoli thought, considering his own history. His case was not as bad as others the doctor had seen, especially at the VA clinic, but still, Nathan had needed help. Even now, he was not certain that his friend was en-tirely cured. He seemed fine, but a relapse was always pos-sible, given the right circumstances, the right conditions. Albert knew that his friend spent a lot of time tramping through the woods alone, but Nathan had always loved the woods, so the doctor thought his hikes were a good thing, a form of natural therapy. Nathan's biggest problem was the hallucinations. It had taken Rizzoli some time to finally convince Nathan that his mind was playing tricks on him, that the fantastic images he saw were mental phantoms and nothing more. Thank God that was over.

It was a clear night but in the black woods, it was dark as a cave. He had no visual landmarks to guide him. but he sensed that he was almost down from the mountain. The road curved sharply to the right and he headed into the curve, thinking how nice it would be to sit with a Bailey's on the rocks once he got home, but the road ahead suddenly exploded in a flash of green light that blinded him. He felt his fingers lift off the steering wheel, felt the car lurch fur-ther right as gravel sprayed up, pinging off the sides of the car and the headlights seemed to go cock-eyed as they lit up not the rutted road but, at first, nothing but the flash of light but then, a luminous figure, a man that seemed to be made of green crystal and shot through with tiny flickering lights and he knew the car was heading toward the figure, was, in fact, driving through it, and then the headlights dipped at a crazy angle, his body slamming forward against the steering column and the lights bounced once off the trees and the rocks at the edge of Bonney Brook far below and that was the last thing he ever saw.

"You really don't need to stay here, Nathan," Leslie said. "She's sound asleep. Why don't you go home and get some rest yourself?"

He sat up taller in the chair beside the couch. "No, I'm fine. Really," he said, doing his best to stifle a yawn.

"You're like a knight in shining armor, aren't you?" she said, smiling. "Protecting the fair damsels from the dragon."

"I guess so." He grinned sheepishly. "That's how I roll."

"It's cute."

"Maybe it is, but there might really be a dragon out there. You know that, don't you?"

"Yes, and I appreciate your wanting to take care of us, I really do." She looked out the window to where the rail of the deck was visible in the porch light like a line of pickets, beyond that nothing but darkness. "I do wish this was all over."

He nodded. "So do I."

"Do you really think Kevin was murdered?"

"Yes."

"I was hoping that maybe you would change your mind."

"I wish I could, believe me." Truly, he didn't need to be caught up in such drama. He had had enough of that in Iraq. But what was he to do? He couldn't simply leave the women on their own, not when he knew what he knew. There were things in those woods that defied logic, that defied rational thought. It didn't matter whether one believed in them, they were there. The nightmare was real. He had seen it.

He watched Sandy sleeping on the couch. She looked peaceful now as she lay there, a strand of her blonde hair resting across her cheek. No nightmares troubled her sleep, he hoped, and he would do whatever was within his power to see that no nightmares bedeviled her daylight hours either. She deserved better.

"You're in love with her, aren't you?" Leslie said, interrupting his reverie.

"What?" he said, flustered, realizing that she had been watching him watch Sandy. "In love?"

She laughed. "If you could only see your face right now. You're red as a beet."

"Come on, Leslie."

"Don't worry about it," she said, with a wave of her hand. "It will be our little secret. Although Sandy's not stupid and you're pretty obvious."

He didn't say anything more; what could he say? He and Sandy didn't have a relationship—they hardly knew each other, really—yet he could not deny the feelings that rose within him simply looking at her. He was not impetuous in matters of the heart. If anything, he was too cautious, too afraid to take risks. Everyone gets burned in love, at least one time and his time had come with Elaine, a college girl-friend who, after one serious, hot and heavy year with him went back to her former boyfriend, a guy Nathan never even knew existed, a guy to whom she had once been engaged. Nathan thought she had been the woman he could stay with forever and acted that way, giving her whatever she wanted. How could he have been so wrong?

The breakup occurred only one month before graduation. Nathan, completely unprepared for a rocky job market with a bachelor's degree in natural resources management, and still smarting from Elaine's betrayal, decided the military was as good a place for him as any. Wrong again.

But the problem with Sandy was that she was like sun-shine on butter, melting away the reserve he had been so carefully cultivating since Elaine. She had no idea, of course, that she was doing that—she wasn't a tease—but the effect was the same. He found himself wanting to know more about her, wanting to confide in her, to share secrets with her, wanting simply to be in her radiant presence. Was that love? If so, then yes, he loved her. He had no idea what she thought about him if she thought about him at all, but sometimes their eyes met, and it seemed to him there were hidden messages transmitted in her gaze. Still, considering all that was going on around them, this was hardly the time to profess his love. Nor was it the time to respond to Leslie's jests.

"Have you two reconsidered coming down into town?" he asked, hoping she would allow him to change the subject.

She glanced out the back windows again before turning to him. "My father built this house many years ago and he and I spent happy times here. You know that. It's my house now, Nathan." He waited for her to continue. "It's my house," she repeated, softly. "But I'm not an idiot. If we need to be in a safer place for a while, then so be it."

"I'm glad to hear that. When?"

"Soon. Let's have Doctor Rizzoli look at her and then we'll come into town."

"So, another day, maybe two, tops?" She nodded. "Okay, but I'm staying with you two until then."

"That's hardly . . ."

"Forget it, Leslie, I've made up my mind. I'm staying. I'll sack out on the couch or, if you don't want that, I'll sleep out in my truck, but in any case, I'm staying."

"You're something."

"The knight in shining armor, remember?"

That night he slept on the floor by the doors to the back deck since Sandy was still asleep on the couch and Leslie slept in her own bedroom. The loft bed was empty, but he felt he should be closer to the women, just in case.

Lying there on the floor he did not feel like a knight. The knight recognized his foes—dragons, rogue knights, infidels—but this enemy was faceless and unknown. Or was it? What about the Spirit Eater? Was there really such a being? Albert had warned him about hallucinations, but his dead dog had been no hallucination. And what about the weird history of this place? Dudleytown was certainly an accursed place, but how did he know if there was a curse at work here? The village could just have been one of those places where unlucky things happened to unlucky people, like in Iraq where he had seen innocent people blown away in the wrong place at the wrong time. Nothing but dumb luck working there. No, he did not have the clear-eyed certainty of the knight for whom good and evil were as distinguishable as black and white.

He was restless. He threw back the light blanket Leslie had given him, quietly opened the door to the deck and stepped out. With the backlight off the darkness was at first impenetrable. Gradually, his eyes adjusted, and he was able to discern the darker shadows of trees beyond the deck. The air was cool, the night quiet. He lifted his head and looked straight up. The surrounding forest made it seem like he was looking through a spy-glass, with the moon a white pearl caught in the circle of darkness. He returned his gaze to the woods, the image of the moon still floating in his vision for a few seconds. Hard as he might try he could not peer into the heart of the forest. He had the unnerving feeling that something was peering back at him. It could see him, but he could not see it.

There had been a night like that in the desert. There had been many nights like that, he thought, but one in particular that he remembered well. Behind rocks and sandbags, he looked into the vast darkness of the desert and saw nothing. His night-vision goggles only made the darkness green, but nothing disturbed the scene. So, why did he have the sensation that someone was watching him? It was like an itch he could not scratch. He remembered his relief Pfc. Stanton coming up beside him. Still, he felt they were being watched. He turned to Stanton and was about to whisper something to him when he heard the crack and ping and saw a black hole suddenly open up in Stanton's neck just above his armor, saw the look of surprise on his face as Stanton crumpled to the ground and then all Hell broke loose.

That's how he felt now. Something was watching. Something was coming. He only hoped that he would be better prepared this time.

Sandy awoke late the following morning. Still groggy, she sat up on the couch and swung her legs over to the floor. Outside, a small patch of sunlight glowed in the clearing beyond the deck and that cheered her. She heard voices in the kitchen. She pushed herself to her feet and shuffled into the kitchen.

Leslie and Nathan looked up at her from where they sat at the table drinking coffee.

"How are you feeling, sweetie?" Leslie asked.

"Like I've been asleep for a thousand years. What time is it, anyway?"

"Just past ten," Nathan said.

"Are you hungry? Would you like something to eat?" Leslie said as Sandy seated herself at the table.

She shook her head. "Just coffee."

Nathan studied her while Leslie got up to fill a cup for her. She still looked tired, he thought, despite all that sleep No doubt that was a result of the sedative Albert had given her. He knew from experience about the drug hangover. He looked at her eyes which seemed to have a little more sparkle to them than they did yesterday, but she still did not seem to him to be one hundred percent. Albert would be able to give him a better perspective once he did his workup.

Leslie set the cup on the table. Sandy wrapped both hands around it, staring vacantly at it for a few seconds before slowly raising it to her lips.

"Are you feeling any better?" Leslie said.

Of course not, Nathan thought. She didn't just have some garden variety headache. She was on the verge of something more serious. He was no psychiatrist but his own experience and what he had seen in Iraq told him that she needed help. But he could forgive Leslie's simplistic question, coming as it did from a friend who cared for her but didn't know how to help her.

She took a few sips from the cup before returning it to the table. She idly brushed a strand of hair from her face. "I need a shower."

"Yes, go right ahead," Leslie said. "We're not going anywhere."

She went up to the loft for clean clothes and a few minutes later, they heard the water running in the shower.

"We need to call Doctor Rizzoli," Leslie said.

"Yes, I was just thinking about that." He took his cell phone out of his pocket and called the doctor. As usual, the doctor's receptionist Rita answered the phone. She was distraught.

"Oh, Nathan, haven't you heard?" Between sobs, she told him that the doctor's car had been found early that morning nose-down in Bonney Brook. "Albert is dead."

He closed his phone and sat there, stunned. Sadness and anger welled up in him simultaneously. He was grieved to lose a friend, enraged that there was yet another death on the mountain. "Fuck! Fuck! Fuck!" he said, slamming the phone on the table repeatedly until it finally shattered in his hand.

"Nathan! What is it?" Leslie said.

He calmed down long enough to tell her what had happened.

"Oh, God!"

"Right."

No one spoke, the only sound coming from the shower in the bathroom.

"What now?"

"Damned if I know." He tapped his fingers on the table, flicking off a piece of broken plastic. "I just can't believe it. Albert was a good friend."

"I'm sorry." They heard the shower turn off. "What about Sandy? What do we do?"

"We'll have to find someone else. I still think she needs help."

"Do we tell her what happened?"

He shook his head. "No, I don't think so. She was already asleep when Albert said he would come back, so she doesn't know that was what he had planned. I'm afraid if she hears about one more person dying, she'll go over the edge."

"I'm about ready to go over the edge myself."

EIGHTEEN

The memory of the man in the wrecked car plagued Sweet-Boy, stalking him like a ghost. He laughed bitterly at that, one "ghost" stalking another. But, in truth, wasn't that happening? The Spirit Eater was out there, and it was all Sweet-Boy could do to stay one step ahead of him. If only he could find the way to where he belonged. Surely, he wasn't meant to be stranded here on this mountain for all eternity. What had he done to deserve such a fate? Why would God—was it God?—do such a thing to him?

He remembered drifting among the hemlocks above the creek, trying to become just one more shadow in the dark woods, one little whisper in the creaking branches. He wished he could shrink himself to the size he was when he was a baby—so long ago now—smaller even, shrink himself to a little ball of light that would once and for all finally wink out like a candle caught in a gust of wind. But no, it was not to be and there he was, twisting in the night breeze like a flimsy kite.

As though his eyes had only just opened he became aware of a dim yellow glow emanating up from the creek bed. Trembling—was it merely the night wind or something else that chilled him?—he moved toward the light. Part of him resisted. He seemed to hear a voice in his head screaming, *Go back! Go back!* Still, he went on.

He heard the black water of Bonney Brook gurgling over the rocks as he descended into the creek bed. The water swirled around the silver vehicle that had dived into the brook from the road above. The front was crumpled like paper, jammed into the rocks, but one light was still intact, shining just below the surface of the water. Two moths danced over the water, attracted by the light.

Sweet-Boy saw the steep slope above the vehicle marred by its wild descent. Deep furrows cut through the weeds and a few saplings had been snapped in half. Leaves draped the vehicle and a large tree limb lay across the roof.

He drew nearer to the vehicle, all the while pushing down his fear. Heat radiated from it in steamy wisps and he heard a soft metallic *ping, ping* coming from the front. The large glass window at the front of the vehicle was shattered. It looked as though a thousand spiders had spun their webs there.

He moved through the water, never feeling its cold, and went around to the other side of the vehicle. There, the battered door was thrown open. A bloodied man lay sprawled on his back, his legs and hips twisted beneath the wheel inside the vehicle, his chest and head hanging out of the vehicle against the wet rocks. Blood painted his face, streamed through his hair and found its way to the water flowing beneath his head. Sweet-Boy drifted closer. The man's open mouth made it seem as though he still screamed. The eyes were open as well and staring and when Sweet-Boy gazed into the dead man's eyes and saw the horror reflected there— a horror he knew only too well—he felt an icy jolt of panic surge through him and suddenly he was away from there, huddled somewhere in a tangled thicket far from the brook.

He drew his knees up to his chest, trying to make himself as small as possible for it seemed to him the woods were too deep for him now and worse, they gave shelter to the Spirit Eater. He felt like an outcast in a place he had once called home. He longed for the security of his shack in the ravine, the comforting solidity of the gravestone at the rear but he no longer trusted that place. Surely, Spirit Eater was everywhere; he would be there as well. He cried without tears—for what ghost had tears?—crying piteously for himself left all alone here with the demonic ghost.

But was he really alone? What about the others? Lady, Yellow Lady, and the Mountain Man were still on the mountain. He had not been able to communicate with Yellow Lady, that was true, but he still felt she had an unexplainable hold upon him. Somehow, she was magic, and her magic had something to do with him being a prisoner on this mountain. She had forged an invisible chain that linked them. He was powerless to break free of it.

He had the sense events were swirling around him, like the waters swirling around the wrecked vehicle. He saw faces from his former life and the faces of the present all mingling together timelessly, without any differentiation, any recognition of past or present. This place was now, he was now, everything was now. He didn't know how it could be, but Yellow Lady connected all these things, the spider at the center of the web. Witchlike, she may have set them all into motion.

He felt her calling him, not as he had once heard things, but in a more visceral way that resonated within him, as though Yellow Lady herself was inside him, just as the poor captured souls of his victims were inside Spirit Eater. He should be with her now.

Cautiously but quickly, he had found his way back to the house on Dark Entry Road. From the safety—not quite as safe as before—of the woods behind the house he watched. A narrow swath of moonlight streaked across the roof of the house, otherwise swaddled in darkness. Nothing moved. The house looked unoccupied to Sweet-Boy's eyes, but something tugged at him and told him, *Stay, I am here.* It was Yellow Lady.

Darkness meant little to him and he clearly saw the door to the deck open and a man step out. He recognized Mountain Man. The man looked up at the moon and then out to the woods and Sweet-Boy was sure the man looked directly at him. Again, something flashed within Sweet-Boy and he knew Mountain Man, like himself, was a prisoner of Yellow Lady, caught in her magic.

With his dying breath, the sachem Namquid had summoned it from out of the darkness. Once brought forth into the world of men it welcomed the spirit of the sachem and received it, taking on his power as its own. With the spirit of Namquid in control, it stalked through Dudleytown, seeking revenge, hunting down those who had murdered the sachem. But once unleashed, it could not be banished again to the darkness. It continued to feed upon the murderers and once they were gone, to feed upon their children and their children's children, swallowing their screaming spirits, feeding upon their life forces, until at last, Dudleytown was no more. Then did Spirit Eater sleep but it lingered still, deep within the woods hidden and quiescent, waiting.

There had been none who knew the ancient mysteries, none who had the courage to look the ghost in the eyes to release the trapped spirits and thus, draw off its power. For that was the only way that it could be defeated and banished back to the darkness for all time, a powerless ghost, empty as a bag of air.

Spirit Eater slept, but as hibernating squirrels rouse to the rising temperatures of spring, it awoke once more when people returned to the mountain. They were few and far between, young and foolish, and it dispatched some quickly, letting others escape too terrified to ever return and warning everyone to stay off Coltsfoot Mountain. One man, though, defied Spirit Eater and built a house on the mountain. The battle for his spirit was long and hard, but in the end, it too was captured for eternity when he shot himself in the woods. But his daughter and the others remained; that could not stand.

It had recently and quite easily taken the spirit of the man in the brook and, before that, had slaughtered the man—evil as itself—that attacked the woman at the house in the woods. That black spirit was strong with hate, boosting, even more, the power of Spirit Eater. Now had come the time for it to cleanse the mountain of the interlopers, once and for all.

"Here, let me take that," Nathan said, as Leslie came out of her bedroom with a small suitcase. "I'll put it in the truck. Where's Sandy?"

"She's upstairs getting her things together. She'll be down in a minute."

Couldn't be too soon, he thought. After hearing the sad news about Albert, Nathan and Leslie had decided they should all go back into town where they would be safer and closer to help for Sandy. She didn't resist. Nathan still believed that she needed to be in the care of a doctor, at least for a little while, but he also thought that being back in West Cornwall would be a positive change for her.

"Be right back," he said, lugging the suitcase out the door.

He felt it as soon as he stepped outside, that unnerving sense that something was not right. The hairs on his arms rose and his ears strained to hear . . . what? Just as the night before, he had the feeling that someone was watching him. He walked to the truck warily, his eyes darting to the woods around him. Nothing. Yet, it felt to him as though the forest was holding its breath, waiting. The very air around him felt thick, heavy with tension, like Iraq all over again. Beads of sweat formed on his brow. The suitcase nearly slipped from his sweaty grasp.

He reached the truck, tossed the suitcase in the bed, and hurried back to the house.

"Are you alright?" Leslie asked. "You look pale."

"I'm fine. Where is she?"

He had no sooner asked that when she appeared in the doorway carrying a small duffel bag. She gave him a weak smile. "I'm here."

He was glad to see that after her shower she had made an effort to work on her appearance, always a good sign in someone who was depressed. She wore denim shorts and a white, short-sleeved blouse that buttoned up the front; he tried not to pay attention to the vee-shaped neckline. Her hair was washed and pulled back in a ponytail, a shining golden mane beneath the Yankees cap. She looked beautiful.

"Okay, let's go," he said.

He took her duffel from her and the three of them exited the house, Leslie locking the door behind them. If the women felt the same depressing atmosphere that made him nervous, they never showed it. But, no, it was real enough, he thought.

The women climbed into the cab while he stowed the duffel in the bed of the truck. Then, he got behind the wheel and closed the door. He turned the key in the ignition. The engine started to turn over, but then quit. He tried it again. The engine groaned but refused to turn over.

"What's the matter?" Leslie asked. He stopped turning the key and looked at her. "Sorry, dumb question."

He tried one last time without success. "Damn!" He got out of the truck and popped the hood. Everything looked normal. He wiggled the battery cables, but they seemed tightly connected. Besides, it was a brand-new battery, purchased only a few weeks ago. Whatever the problem was, it wasn't anything obvious.

"Leslie," he said, through the window of the truck, "do you have the keys to the Cherokee with you?"

"Of course, right here in my purse."

"Let me have them."

She passed them through the window to him.

He didn't like this at all. He always took good care of his vehicles. There was no reason why his truck should be acting up like that. He walked over to the Jeep, got in and turned the ignition. Nothing but the sickening *click* of the key. Again. Nothing but dead silence.

He got out of the Jeep but didn't bother to check under the hood. It would be worthless effort. Sandy's blue BMW was parked a few feet away. It was worth a shot, even though he already had the sinking feeling that it would not start either. Sure enough, after getting the keys from her, he found the car was as dead as the others. Three dead batteries on three different vehicles. What were the odds of that being coincidental? Astronomical.

He stood by the BMW, feeling as powerless as the dead batteries. The woods seemed closer now that they had no way out, the air heavier than before. *What the hell was going on?* It was as though something had completely drained the batteries. How could that be? His scalp prickled, and the beads of sweat were now beginning to trickle down his face. The palms of his hands were damp. He saw the women in the truck looking at him anxiously. Stay cool, he thought, stay cool. They need you.

He returned to the truck, fighting the urge to turn around to see whatever it was he sensed was watching him. "Come on, girls, back inside. Quickly."

They saw the concern written upon his face and didn't ask any questions as they reentered the house.

"All three batteries? That's impossible," Leslie said, after he had explained the situation to them.

"I know. Look, you two stay here in the house. I'm going to go back out and take a look at the truck again." He really didn't want to go out there but didn't know what else to do. "Maybe I missed something."

"Fine, you can try," said Leslie, pulling her cell phone out of her purse. "While you're doing that, I'm going to call triple A. I've never had to use my membership before, but I know they can jump a dead battery."

She tried to turn on the phone. "That's funny."

"What?" Sandy said.

"I can't get a connection. Try yours."

Sandy took out her phone and flipped it open. She pushed a few buttons. "Dead."

"Let's try the landline," Nathan said. He was standing near the old wall phone in the kitchen and picked up the receiver. He heard only dead air and replaced the receiver. He didn't need to tell the women that the phone was dead.

No vehicles and no way of contacting the outside world. It was as though they had suffered some power blackout. But what kind of blackout affected batteries as well as electrical circuits?

They had to get off the mountain. "Okay, I'm going to try the truck again."

The dense air outside smothered him. He felt it pressing all around. His heart jack-rabbited inside his chest. This was not good. He sweated profusely now. His hands shook as he once again lifted the hood of the truck. He caught the smell of oil and, for a moment, he felt like he was in Iraq standing by a twisted, burnt-out Humvee, oil slimy with blood running into the sand. He shook his head and the vision disappeared. Before him was the cold dead engine of his truck.

He labored to breathe as he examined the engine, his pulse racing. *Shit!* There just wasn't anything that he could see wrong with the engine. It had to be a dead battery. He reached out one more time to tug on the battery cable. Then he stopped.

He felt intense cold surround him. It was as though a block of ice had instantly descended upon him. At the same time the air turned green, an electric buzz shivered his bones. The green, the green, he remembered that, saw again in his mind his dead dog and the ghost—he *knew* it was a ghost moving off through the woods—and now, as he lifted his head from the engine and it seemed like he lifted it very slowly, he saw that same figure, saw the massive war club raised high and he pulled away from the engine, banging his head hard against the raised hood, and he turned away from the thing, from the ghost, never seeing more than the glowing arm and club and he did not know if the club had struck him, or if the hood had knocked him sideways, but he saw the ground rushing up to meet his face, felt the thud and heard something crack somewhere inside him before the green was gone and there was nothing but black.

"What's taking him so long?" Leslie said, pacing the floor. "We need to get out of here." Sandy's worried expression stopped her short. "Don't worry, Sandy, we'll be fine. I promise."

"Okay."

"I'm going to check on him. I'll be right back."

"Les. . . "

"It's alright; I'll just be a minute."

She felt the air thick as molasses the moment she stepped out the door. "What the hell?" She saw Nathan's truck, the hood up, but no Nathan. Where had he gone? She stepped closer to the truck and felt her bare arms go pimply with goosebumps. Something wasn't right. She leaned against the door and looked through the open window. Empty.

"Hello, Leslie."

She felt her blood turn to ice. She knew that voice, even though now it sounded rough and slurred.

Kevin.

She whirled around and there he was, although what she saw was not quite Kevin, but a macabre simulacrum of him. She stood transfixed by fear as she watched the thing that was Kevin but not Kevin mutate back and forth from Kevin to the form of an Indian, body parts pulsing and changing at random so that the thing was hardly recognizable as either one or the other. The thing cast a green glow all around while little shimmering lights shot through it.

She took a step back. "What the fuck!" she whispered.

"Bitch," said the guttural voice that she recognized as Kevin and, yes, for a moment there was Kevin's perverse leer on the face of the thing.

It took her a few seconds to find her feet, but when she did she was already too late, as the thing's arm shot out and grabbed her by the neck and she felt the strong fingers close around her throat, so cold, so cold, and the green glow washed over her while the face only inches from her own was now so clearly Kevin's and he was grinning and his other hand came up to roughly maul her breasts.

"Bitch," the Kevin-thing said again.

She felt the fingers squeeze even tighter around her throat, felt the blood pounding in her head. She could not scream but she clawed at the thing until her fingernails broke. It was as though she had not even touched it. Her feet dangled in the air as the Kevin-thing lifted her off the ground and she felt faint as black spots danced before her eyes, and she heard her clothes ripping off her body, felt them fall off her in tatters, and then the thing slammed her body up against the truck and she felt an intense cold penetrate her and the Kevin-thing grunting in her ear and then it was over, although Spirit Eater didn't stop, even after she was dead.

NINETEEN

She sat on the edge of the couch anxiously waiting for Leslie to return. She had only been gone for a few minutes, but those minutes seemed like an eternity to her. What was keeping her? She didn't like being alone. Unable to sit still any longer, she got up and went to the kitchen window, pushing the curtain aside to look out.

Nightmares have a way of shutting down all the brain's defense mechanisms. All the dreamer can do is watch the horror as it takes hold of her and pray that she will wake soon before she is lost forever. Outside the window, Sandy's daylight nightmare unfolded before her eyes. Part of her brain was screaming at her *run!* while another part tried to make sense of what her eyes were seeing, tried to put the horrific scene into the proper pigeonhole, but in a few seconds that part of her brain gave up and the other part of her brain caused her to scream and forced her feet to move. Blindly, she ran to the back of the house. In a heartbeat, she was on the deck, sprinting toward the woods.

She knew what she had seen, but she was on automatic pilot now and her instinct for survival had taken over. Now, all she could do was think about saving herself; there was no room for other thoughts.

She dashed across the clearing at the rear of the house and crashed into the woods, brambles and branches scratching her arms and legs. She did not know where she was going; only that she was running, running. The irony of running for safety into the deep woods that had so frightened her before was not lost on her, but she would gladly accept that fear over the certain death that would be hers had she remained at the house.

She gulped for air as she ran, her legs burned. There were no paths in the woods. The terrain was rough and uneven, causing her to stumble several times. If she fell or twisted her ankle it would be all over for her, so she tried to slow down enough to see better where she was running.

She lost the sense of time, it felt to her like she had been running for years. She was tiring, slowing down. She couldn't go much further without resting first. The ground began to slope downward, and she soon found herself at the edge of a wooded ravine. She paused and leaned against a tree, panting for air.

She looked down into the ravine. Lost beneath the trees, the ravine was dark with shadows, but as her eyes scanned it, she thought she detected wooden planks. Carefully, she descended into the ravine, holding on to the trees as she made her way down the steep slope and, yes, she was right. Someone had built a rough shack there.

She drew closer to the shack, her heart thumping. The shack seemed to grow out organically from the slope and was partly concealed by bushes. A weathered piece of plywood served as a door. She stopped and listened but heard no sound from within. She crept up to the side and cautiously leaned against it to spy through a chink in the wood. All was dark inside but as her eye adjusted to the darkness it seemed that the shack was empty. Even so, she was careful as she went around to the front of the shack and slid the plywood back a few inches. The shack was empty. She did not hesitate but sought shelter inside.

Sweet-Boy felt powerless. The last wisps of green mist were dissipating in the air when he arrived at the house, but he knew Spirit Eater had been there. Sweet-Boy found Mountain Man first, half concealed in tall weeds at the edge of the woods, lying on his side. Sweet-Boy saw the bloody gash at the side of his head, but the man's eyelids fluttered, and Sweet-Boy noted the shallow rise and fall of his chest.

A truck sat in the driveway, the hood up. It was painted in blood and gore. More blood pooled on the gravel, forming a pond around the naked body of Lady, or what used to be Lady. He stood there staring at the body, unable to tear his eyes away although he wanted to and felt profound sadness and more. Anger. It rose up in him, hotly burning and he heard the voices of all the others, the trapped souls crying out to him again.

Then he remembered; where was Yellow Lady? Panicked, he was instantly inside the house seeking her out, but she was not there. Gone. Had Spirit Eater taken her? She would already be dead if the ghost had her. No, she was alive. She must be. But where was she? Where?

He stood on the deck at the rear of the house, head tilted, listening. The energy, the vibrations of all that surrounded him pulsed through his body. The essence of every living thing surged through him and he waited, waited, hoping to detect that special vibration that emanated from Yellow Lady. But he did not have much time. Where was she?

He lifted off the deck and was halfway through the clearing when he felt it, a searing jolt that speared through his body with such intensity it was almost painful. It lasted only a moment and then was gone, Yellow Lady reaching out to him. He paused in the clearing, turning slowly, his body alive with sensation as though a million spiders crawled upon it, and then again, there it was, this time a few seconds duration. He turned in the direction from which he thought the vibrations flowed and drifted toward them and, yes, they grew stronger and lasted longer. It was as though Yellow Lady had thrown him a lifeline. He focused all his attention on that stream of energy and quickly followed down the path it had blazed through the dark woods.

She fell onto the old mattress in the shack, exhausted. The damp mattress stank, but at that moment, it felt like a mattress from one of the swankiest hotels in Manhattan. Thin trickles of blood ran upon her arms and legs where tree branches and thorns had savaged her. She had lost her hat somewhere in the woods and her hair was wild, plucked by the woody fingers of tree limbs as she darted beneath them. Her heart burned and it was all she could do to catch a breath.

Now that she had stopped running, her mind turned to the grisly scene outside her door. Despite her best efforts to block it out, to think of something else, anything else, she saw her friend's mangled body wrapped python-like in a green mist that looked human at times, looked, in fact, like. . . Kevin! *But he's dead!* her rational mind screamed, while the other part of her mind—the dark, animal part that lay hidden deep within her mental jungle—replied, *And your point?* She shuddered and drew her knees up against her chest, clasping them tightly, trying to make herself as small as possible in the nightmare surrounding her.

Think, Sandy! She pushed through the monsters in her mind, clinging to her like spider webs. No time for them now. She looked around, finally noticing the little table and the candle, the blanket that hung on the rear wall and the white stone—a tombstone?—that stood before it. She examined the slab more closely and saw the letters chiseled into it. Yes, a tombstone, although she had no idea why it would be in the shack. Her heart froze. Sitting just below the tombstone, half-hidden in shadow was the TotToy teddy bear that had gone missing from the house. She didn't remember when she noticed it was gone, but she hadn't seen it for a few days.

Who owned this place? More importantly, was he friend or foe? She couldn't stick around to find out. She had to take her chances. Whoever owned this place knew her. She had to get off the mountain. Slowly, she rose to her feet. Taking a couple of deep breaths to calm her rapid-fire heart, she took hold of the plywood sheet and pushed it open.

Nathan forced his eyes open. The left eye, sticky with blood, took more effort. Vertical green bars appeared directly before him. It took him a few seconds to recognize that he was lying on his side in the tall weeds. What was he doing there? His mind cleared and he remembered the green arm and the war club slicing down through the air, remembered the blow—but was it the club, or the hood of the truck?—and hitting the ground, instinctively rolling off into the relative safety of the weeds before he lost consciousness.

His head throbbed. When he lifted a hand to touch it, his fingers came away bloody. Okay, but he was alive. Slowly, he pushed himself up to a sitting position, his head spinning as he moved upright. He tried to push off on his left arm to raise himself to a standing position but when he did, something sharp stabbed through his forearm and he collapsed upon it, wincing in pain. *Shit! Fractured!* He remembered hearing an ominous *crack* as he hit the ground. Levering himself up on his right side, he finally stood on both feet.

Even before he saw the body, the sickly-sweet smell of blood came to him, an odor he had smelled all too often in Iraq. He saw his truck, now dripping with a new coat of crimson and when he drew closer, saw what was left of Leslie. He fell back against the truck, biting back the bile he felt rising within him. *Jesus Christ!* It wasn't as though he hadn't seen dead bodies before but what the Spirit Eater—he was sure now of his ghost—had done to her was far more horrific than anything he had seen on the battlefield. The horror lay in the cruel deliberateness of her death, a careful torture and execution that could only be called demonic.

He staggered away from the corpse, favoring his painful left arm. Where was Sandy? He looked around but saw no sign of her. The house? He opened the door and went inside, but it was obvious in only a few moments that she was not there, nor was there any evidence of violence in the house. He saw the door to the deck standing ajar. He walked out onto the deck. Nothing. Where could she have gone? And where was Spirit Eater?

What to do, what to do; his mind was frantic with worry. He ran, as best he could, out into the clearing behind the house, searching the periphery, looking for something, anything that would help him find her. He stopped, panting, his head swimming. Then he saw it. Just beyond a patch of weeds that looked as though something had dragged through it, a spot of dark blue. He forged through the thicket and found Sandy's Yankees cap hung up on the brambles of a blackberry bush.

He stood there, her cap in his hand, and examined the bushes around him, looking for her path. He saw where the grasses were pushed flat, and branches bent aside and decided that was the way to go. He felt adrenaline rushing through his body and the pain in his head subsided. There was little time left before Spirit Eater found her if he hadn't already. *Don't think that way, it can't happen.* He pushed through the bushes, following her trail, his eyes alert to new twists and turns. He would find her.

It moved swiftly through the forest, energized by the new spirit it had taken, feeling its strength increasing by the moment. But the work was not yet finished; people still remained on the mountain. And there was something else, something not human. Spirit Eater had already suspected that presence, had detected its weak vibrations before, but whatever it was, it lacked power, it was not a threat.

Tendrils of glowing green mist swirled in its wake as Spirit Eater flew through the woods, seeking, seeking. It knew how strong the life force was and it knew it would eventually detect that force, homing in on the vibrations, until at last, the prey was discovered. It would not be long.

Nothing could escape it now. Nothing.

The trail was easy to follow, even for someone lacking in his knowledge of the woods. It was obvious to him that Sandy was terrified, running blindly without direction through the woods that to her were unknown and fearsome territory. He could imagine what she felt as she fled to the woods all alone, the memory of her best friend's body fresh in her mind. He had already been worried about her state of mind, what would this do to her? He wished he was with her now, wished he could hold her, comfort her, and let her know she was not alone; he was with her, would always be with her.

He cursed the fractured arm that hindered his progress through the underbrush. Still, he pushed on as best he could, as quickly as he could, keenly aware that every passing second could be bringing her that much closer to death.

He ran through the woods. An owl hooted, Nathan's mind registering the mournful sound almost as an afterthought. His breathing was ragged, and he became aware of a thickening in the air, just as he had felt back at the house, and he knew what that signaled. His eyes darted as he ran, hoping to catch a glimpse of the glowing green ghost before it saw him, but there was nothing. Yet, the air grew denser. It was close.

I'm coming Sweet-Boy mentally telegraphed to Yellow Lady. He did not know whether she would hear him, but he thought she would; she was magic. Her vibrations were strong and visible to him now as slender strands of gold gleaming in the darkness of the woods. He felt like a fish being reeled in by those beautiful lines. The energy he absorbed riding those strands coursed through him and he had never felt so strong, so alive—an odd thought—so powerful. It was her magic. She was sending him her magic.

He knew the forest well and he recognized the sloping hillside immediately. He had abandoned it out of fear that Spirit Eater would catch him there, but now, as he caught a glimpse of the familiar shack nestled in the ravine, he felt no fear. No, he did not because Yellow Lady awaited him there.

Nathan felt the ground beneath his feet begin to angle downward and suddenly he came to the edge of a ravine, a place he had never seen before despite his familiarity with the forest. The sides sloped steeply, and he could see where someone had slid down through the trees and bushes that marched up the ravine.

"Sandy!" he called, unafraid now to make noise when seconds mattered. The air was growing thicker by the minute and he thought he detected a glowing tinge of green in the distance. "Sandy! Are you there?"

He peered into the bottom of the deeply shadowed ravine. Was there something moving down there? He crab-walked down a few steps, grabbing onto trees with his right arm as he went. He heard something cutting through the air above him. He looked up in time to see two white owls fly by and perch in the trees overhead. A third joined the pair seconds later. That rare sight stopped him momentarily. He looked back down and called once more, "Sandy!"

She thought she heard someone calling her name. She scrambled out of the shack. Yes, there it was again.

"Nathan?" she yelled.

She looked up but could not see anyone. The air was leaden. It felt like someone had thrown a heavy blanket over her. A strange light filtered down into the ravine like smoke. It seemed to glow. She heard something shuffling around in the bushes above her but still could not see anyone.

The light began to coalesce, glowing brighter. Shot through with sparkling lights, it was shaping itself into human form. She wanted to scream, but she could not find her voice. Her long nightmare continued as she watched arms and legs form out of the glowing mass until the figure of an Indian carrying a war-club stood before her, but not for long, as it shape-shifted into Kevin.

Now she screamed.

Before she could run, Kevin backhanded her across the face, a blow that felt like an electric jolt, and sent her sprawling. She tried to scramble away but the thing that was Kevin grabbed her by the hair and yanked her up to her knees. His face was only inches from her own and she saw the eyes were not the eyes of Kevin, but were deep and black, the eyes of an animal and the face was no longer his either, rippling like wind on water and changing into the Indian. He pulled her head back and she saw above her an owl glide into the ravine and she thought that was not a bad thing to see before she died.

She thought she saw movement from the corner of her eye and turned her head as best she could to see what looked like a little boy standing nearby. Impossible, of course, her brain was shutting down on her, but there he was nonetheless, and she seemed to know him.

He heard the scream and almost threw himself down the ravine to get to her. The air glowed green and in the midst of that greenish cloud, Nathan saw the ghost, Spirit Eater, yank Sandy to her feet by her hair.

Nathan grabbed a stout stick that was lying on the ground and charged the ghost, bellowing like a madman, and he realized perhaps he was mad to think that such a weapon would have any effect on the ghost, but what else was he to do? He swung it wildly at the ghost, but he never made contact with anything solid, the stick slicing through the thing as though it was water.

He struck the ghost again and again, but the thing treated him as though he were a pesky fly, all the while holding Sandy, now with one hand clamped around her neck. Finally, as though bored with the game, the ghost lashed out with his club, catching Nathan across the back of the knees.

It felt to him as though a live wire had sparked through his legs and they crumpled under him. Before he could get up the ghost had taken a step forward, pushing the club against his back, as though impaling him with a spear. The pain was electric and excruciating. There was roaring in his ears and he heard Sandy sobbing and choking and somewhere above him he heard the hooting of owls. His vision grew blurry. He must have been hallucinating, as he saw a little boy walking toward him.

"Stop it!"

Nathan heard the voice, the voice of a child. The club was still pressed against his back, but Nathan sensed the ghost was more interested in something else. The child. He looked again, and the hallucination had not disappeared. Wearing old-fashioned overalls and a plaid shirt, the boy was only a few feet away.

Sweet-Boy stood trembling before Spirit Eater. He called out for it to stop and, for a moment it did, but then it shook Yellow Lady as though she were a rag doll, her head wobbling, the yellow hair rippling like a flag.

"No!" He still felt those golden cords binding him to Yellow Lady, but he sensed they were growing weaker. He must do something. He summoned his courage, the strength Yellow Lady had given him and walked forward, lifting his eyes up to the ghost. It was all he had.

This was the other thing he had sensed, puny and powerless as he had imagined. Spirit Eater dropped Sandy in a heap and turned its attention to the boy. He bent down to get a good look at him before he squashed him like an insect.

Sweet-Boy looked up into the dark, black eyes of Spirit Eater and instantly, a stream of white light sprang from his eyes into the eyes of the ghost. Sweet-Boy felt pain, but not as much as Spirit Eater, who now howled in agony, twisting its body in a futile attempt to pull away from the boy's gaze. It was as though this light-bridge connected them deep within their very souls.

"Come out!" called Sweet-Boy, "Come out!"

Sweet-Boy felt energy flowing into him on that light beam and then, slowly at first, but then more rapidly, little sparkling lights, like fireflies, began flying out from Spirit Eater's eyes.

Nathan rolled out from under the war club and crawled over to Sandy, keeping one eye fixed upon the ghost. She was unconscious but breathing. He held her, and her eyelids finally fluttered open. "Thank god!" He pulled her closer, despite his fractured arm.

Sweet-Boy stood his ground, his eyes fixed on those of Spirit Eater while all around them the air was filled with the captured spirits, now released, winging their way skyward.

Spirit Eater seemed to sag as the spirits left him and his light began to dim.

Nathan and Sandy watched the glittering spirits as they rose up and they noticed for the first time the trees were filled with beautiful white owls. One by one the owls lifted off from the branches and flew into the lights, merging with them in brilliant flashes, flying away then, their white forms dissolving in the dusky sky.

Spirit Eater now resembled an emaciated old man. He no longer fought Sweet-Boy but stood there feebly, still locked onto the boy's unflinching gaze. At last, the light-bridge winked out, as though someone had turned off a switch. Spirit Eater stood there for a moment, looking at the boy in bewilderment, then fell to the ground. A stream of greenish mist squiggled out from his body and dissipated in the air. The body lost all color and disappeared.

Nathan released Sandy and stood, his legs wobbly. The boy remained standing before them, his bare feet looking so childishly pathetic in the dirt. "Thank you," Nathan said.

Sweet-Boy smiled, but he was not smiling at Nathan. His smile was for the two people, a man and a woman, who now stood there, arms open wide for their little boy.

Nathan thought he heard a voice: *My Sweet-Boy, come!*

The boy ran to them, his arms outstretched, and they embraced. In seconds, they were gone, turned into three tiny lights that rode owl escorts up and out of the ravine.

Forever.

EPILOGUE

It is said that time heals all wounds, and, in time, Sandy's wounds were healed. It did not happen quickly, as the deaths of her former lover and best friend were grievous wounds. They required special care from those who were trained to deal with such hurts.

Nathan understood this and waited. Had he not suffered such wounds himself? He was a patient man and he was there for her every day while she recovered. He would never leave her alone again. He would do anything for her.

The first thing he did for her—and for himself as well— was to attend Leslie's funeral in the little cemetery in West Cornwall. There were folks he recognized from the village that came to pay their respects. She was buried beside her father and when Nathan lingered at the graveside following the service, his prayer was for both of them.

Then came the day not long after when he no longer visited Sandy because she walked out from the hospital on his arm. Day by day she grew stronger and at last, the nightmares vanished, Nathan being largely responsible for their banishment.

Still, it was several months before they once again ventured up Coltsfoot Mountain. It was an unusually bright winter's day with a cloudless blue sky. Patches of snow lay in the ravines. The woods were bare, and sunlight striped the hillsides with tree shadows. They parked the car on Cook Road and walked the fifty yards through the frozen grasses to the little cemetery nestled beneath the trees.

There was one small stone lovingly embraced by the root of a tree. The name carved upon it read *Sweet-Boy*. The couple stood hand in hand looking down at the stone. Then, Sandy drew something out of the tote bag she was carrying. She bent down and carefully placed the teddy-bear beside the grave.

"Good-bye, Sweet-Boy," she said, softly, "and thank you."

She took Nathan's hand and rose to her feet. With their arms around each other, they walked back to the car.

They never returned to Dudleytown.

ABOUT THE AUTHOR

JOHN B. KACHUBA is the award-winning author of ten books, five of them about paranormal and metaphysical topics. He is a regular speaker at universities, libraries, and conferences, and has made numerous appearances on TV, radio, and podcasts. For more information, please go to www.johnkachuba.com